THE FAT GIT
The Story of a Merlin

Alan Richardson

SKYLIGHT
PRESS

First published in Great Britain in 2012 by Skylight Press,
210 Brooklyn Road, Cheltenham, Glos GL51 8EA

Designed and typeset by Rebsie Fairholm
Publisher: Daniel Staniforth

Front cover photo by Naomi Banham (photographer) and husband
Mick (Merlin model).
Back cover inset photo by Matt Baldwin-Ives (photographer – see
www.milescross.co.uk) and Guy Brooks (Merlin model).

Printed and bound in Great Britain by Lightning Source, Milton
Keynes

www.skylightpress.co.uk

ISBN 978-1-908011-31-2

DEDICATION

To the urbane and elegant Mark Colmar. We originally wrote this as a film script, and tried to get Robbie Coltrane to play the part of Ambrose Hart, not because of his bulk, but because he can 'do voices'. Alas, we couldn't get near the Great Man because, according to his agent, he was far too busy down Diagon Alley at the time.

I then went behind Mark's back and reverse-engineered our script into this novella, without telling him. After a mature and adult discussion we are now friends again, and the bruising on my testicles has just about gone down…

"*Merlin* was a perennial title, given to magically skilled individuals, rather than a single figure from myth and legend…"

Christine Campbell Thomson

"Inside every Fat Git there's an Enchanter wildly signalling to be let out."

Ambrose Hart

THE FAT GIT
The Story of a Merlin

AMBROSE HART opened the door of his cottage onto a perfect morning. It *had* to be a perfect morning because the whole day, the whole world, was a reflection of himself: his eyes were pale and clear and so was the sky; his complexion was pink and healthy and so were the roses. If his stomach bulged a little – well, more than a little – it was no more than an expression of the hills around the town. By running his fingers back through his hair and adjusting the elastic in his pony tail, he ensured that the town's park would be well-tended and the trees in tip-top condition, while the tattoos on his body provided auguries for the people if only they cared to read them properly. He burped, and ensured the scented breeze that would help the washing dry upon their lines. He farted, and knew that the small petrol station would be *well* stocked that day.

Shuck, his old black dog with long legs and pointy ears, ran past him and reared up onto the low gate, looking back and forth as if to confirm that all was well in the world of Strathnaddair. And so it was, and so it was… birds trilled. A red squirrel came around a bush and noticed the dog, the man, then looked toward the latter for guidance. *Go on*, he said, mind-to-mind, and the creature shot across the grass and up the tree before the dog could notice.

"A fine morning!" said the postman, patting the dog on the head as he walked on past, humming, kicking his legs out in a jaunty walk that suggested he had found True Love and Happiness in the dying moments of the local ceilidh again. "Nothing for you today, you fat bastard!"

It *was* a fine morning, because he, Ambrose Hart, had willed it so. That was part of his job. Plus he had known there would be no post long before the letters had even been sorted for the small market town as a whole – though it wouldn't have done for the wee lad to know that.

He took several deep breaths, hearing the pure air whistle through the hairs in each nostril, and jiggled with his belt against his spreading belly. The day sang, because he wanted it to sing. Turning his head one way and then the next, he was almost certain that the song to which the world thrummed this morning was *Light my Fire* by the Doors. A hopeful song, as he was hopeful himself. Musick, as he thought of it, floated into his mind from another plane. It came to him like the smell of cooking in a large and happy family: he sort of sniffed it in. Whether the musick was inspired *by* the events, or actually *caused* them, was of no concern to Hart. The musick was never celestial, and neither did the lyrics matter: it was all to do with the notes, and their potency, and their ability to fill his innards like food. One of the oddest times in his life was when he kept humming the theme from *Dr Who* every day at 11:11 for a week, and he never fathomed the Mystery behind *that* arcanum.

He picked up the single pint of milk, felt the glass cold and almost wet against his hand, then – making sure with a lifetime of practise that no-one was watching – he did that little thing with his mind and – lo! – there were two pints. An odd talent, but it didn't half save on his bills.

"Shuck! Come on you smelly beast!" he called, and the dog, which seemed to have more facial expression than most humans and certainly more brains, got down on all fours and followed him inside. Before he closed the door he paused on the step, took another look, listened to a few more inner notes of the song and sort of pointed with intent at the earth, the sky, the sun and nearby river, as if jabbing instructions at all the local elements which made up the weather. Which of course he was.

"A fine day, all day. So mote it be," he said softly, but also very firmly, because it didn't do for someone like himself to vacillate. The elementals – tricksy little buggers which took on the fantastical shapes his mind needed – got anxious if he did that. So then the day just *had* to be fine, because underneath the tattooed middle-aged spread, beneath the leather and denim and kick-arse boots of an ageing biker, with his greying ponytail and remnants of attitude, and an admirable collection of vinyl records, Ambrose Hart was quietly cursed and blessed in equal measure as The Merlin of Strathnaddair…

Afternoon, a picnic on one of the hills which sheltered and almost encircled the town. The pink chequered cloth was spread across the grass, items of food were placed on squares as if it were a chess game and meanwhile, with deep feelings of enormous guilt, Ambrose and his sister Yvonne were doing what brothers and sisters have covertly and guiltily done for millennia now – squabbling.

"You've gotta do something about your weight," she said. "Your heart. You can get diabetes. You can —"

"I'm not fat. I've put on a few pounds since I stopped smoking."

"You're fat. What woman in her right mi—"

"I'm not fat, I'm…*Oh*-lympian!" Without looking, as casually as Yvonne flicked ash from her cigarette, he raised his finger and made small lightnings crash, and the way his sister ignored this you knew that it was a very old trick of his. "Anyway, forget about me, look at your son. Look!"

"Oh god," said Yvonne. "How can he…?"

A lithe twelve year old boy called Arthur, her son, was hanging upside down from a tree by one leg, apparently indifferent to anything or anyone, with the violet eyes and noble features you might find painted by the pre-Raphaelites when they were smashed on absinthe.

"*He* can. Anyway, let's finish this shall we?"

Ambrose was happy to change the subject. He was far too busy waving away the tempting smoke from her cigarette, plus chasing off the ants, flies and the occasional salamanders which popped into visible appearance, drawn to the emanations from the golden honey and lashing out with their wicked hooked little tails. Of course being a Merlin he knew that these elementals were more truly seen as pulsating geometric patterns, but where was the fun in seeing them like that, eh? He himself was probably best seen as a series of pulsating geometric patterns, if the truth were told, especially first thing in the morning when he was still in his vest and underpants. He got on well with the gnomes, being an earthy type himself; had a right laugh with the airy sylphs because they were sharp minded like him, and he coped with the moody undines as long as they didn't try to get him into water; but the salamanders…

"Ambrose! Will you help him, *please?* He's your nephew. You gotta do something. Just two nights a week. You *owe* it to him."

He looked, reluctantly. The boy hung perfectly still like the pendulum of a stopped clock, one leg hooked around a branch in an eerie but apparently comfortable fashion, the other one just bent across, arms on his chest and a look of ecstasy on that stupid face of his. Truth was – and he'd die rather than admit it to his sister – he hated the brat, even if they were, according to The Pattern, eternally linked.

"Well?"

He hated this moral blackmail too, and the way his life was supposed to revolve around the boy. Hated the way the sun glinted off his sister's bleached hair, and the low blouse, and the tight jeans that offered lessons in basic gynaecology to any Tom, Dick and Pervy in the village. He hated her rasping voice and sharp tongue and deliberately dog-rough persona. And he hated all these things and more not because he didn't love her, but because they might take away his own guilt, and uncertainty with regard to the boy. He flung the remains of coffee from his cup, the arc of liquid turning into a brief, miniature rainbow; flowers shooting up where it landed.

"I'd say he's doing a remarkably wonderful imitation of *The Hanged Man* from the tarot pack. The Waite/Rider pack that is, not the Crowleyan version that I use. Now according to most interpretations —"

"Stuff that. Gimme a straight answer. When you gonna start teaching him? It's what you do, ye fat bastard. Or s'posed to do. You know that."

He did, and so he did. But the other Merlins in other towns all had normal little Arthurs. Whereas he, The Merlin of

Strathnaddair, arguably the best of them all, got the only autistic, epileptic, malfunctioning once and future king in the whole inner history of royalty. Apart from the Windsors, of course.

"And if you call him an Idiot Savant again I'll stick this knife in yer bloody leg!"

She would too: he moved his leg quickly, and stood up, both to get out of range and give himself time to think. He could spend all day giving himself time to think. Perhaps that was why Strathnaddair was such a sleepy little town.

"*I* never called him that! Blame the Educational Psychologist. Anyway he said *Autistic* Savant. That's a different thing again. I know men who'd give their right testicles to be Autistic Savants."

"Bollocks."

"Exactly!"

Hart went over to his nephew. Angled his own head to look more directly at the boys face. But even after adjusting his perceptions 90 degrees it still looked like ecstasy on the boy's face: the skin had a curious internal shining, not unlike too much hydrocortisone as an infant.

"Wake up you little sod," he said in a near-whisper. "Come and see us someday, or your mam's gonna rip my eyes out. And that thing about me and your dad, honest, I —"

He stopped in mid-sentence. Something had impinged upon his consciousness, very faint but getting stronger. Without realising it he rubbed his palms clean of sweat on his jeans, as if he might be getting a handshake from royalty. The other two had noticed as well: Arthur, still with his silvered eyes, slipped down off the branch in what might have been an uncanny and almost serpentine motion if they had bothered to study it, and Yvonne was up and on her feet, blowing her lungs clear of smoke, stubbing the cigarette out and pushing it into the earth with the low heel of her shoe.

"There," she said, pointing to a tiny speck, getting larger as it circled, spiralled down.

"Here, come to me. Don't be shy. Come to daddy…" muttered Hart, as if afraid to speak too loud in case he scared it away. He scooped up the picnic cloth and scattered everything, wrapping it around his wrist. Arthur, suddenly focused and aware that something special was about to happen, came and stood with his mother. Hart chanted, almost mantrically: "Here, come to me, come to me, to me... come to me quickly, come to me... come to me quickly, come to me..."

The hawk landed on his wrist and flapped its wings for a few beats to steady itself. Hart looked at it closely, into its eyes, communing.

"What is it?" asked Yvonne.

"It's a chicken and mushroom sandwich. It's a bloody *hawk*, woman, what does it look like?"

"I meant the situation, not what sorta creature is it!"

There might have been a row but Arthur spoke then, and they always went silent when he did so, trying to catch his rare words like his uncle had caught the hawk.

"It's a merlin," he said, moving his hands up and down the bird without actually touching it. "A specific type of hawk. *Falco columbarius* is its proper name." This from a boy who never seemed to read anything, just flip through the pages.

Brother and sister look at each other and their faces registered *Ooooooo!* with differing expressions. Yvonne was pleased by her son's erudition; Hart just irritated. Then the older man looked earnestly at the hawk again. He looked into the bird's eyes and through, as if fitting his own eyes into the lenses of binoculars. In his vision he soared as the bird had done, and looked down at a local stone circle surrounded by men in Range Rovers, some with theodolites and maps, all of them in long coats like robes, full of purpose and intent and none of it good. One of them was pissing against the tallest stone.

Closer, the hawk's eyes able to pick out an insect from a million miles, and Hart's spirit vision riding on its back doing similar, and he could see how angry the stone was, the urine steaming gold down its ancient carvings. He could even hear the men talking, bubbles of sound:

"They'll never accept it."

"They already have. I've paid them off."

"The Greens, the loonies..."

"I eat greens. I shit them. I'm a vegetarian. And I'll give the people of Strathwotsit jobs – well, some of them."

"But you'll still use the – er, immigrants?" he asked distastefully.

"Sssh! Not immigrants – cousins. And cheap ones too!"

This man with many cousins got a lot of stick for many things, and most of it deserved, but he didn't have a racist bone in his body. In fact he prided himself on being ruthless with everyone, regardless of race, creed, or colour.

"Still… radioactive waste? Here?" The minion – for he was a politician and hardly deserved an individual name – made a broad gesture which took in the bleakly beautiful hills surrounding them, and the distant rooftops of the town.

"Why not? 'Strathnaddair, The Cider Capital of the World'. A fine place to live – if you're an apple. This is as good a place as any. They'll forgive us – anyway, 'they know not what we do'. And let's keep it that way."

The master buttoned himself up and wiped his hands on a monogrammed handkerchief then handed it to one of his lackeys. He had felt suddenly uneasy, as if he was being spied upon. He shivered briefly, shrugged into his coat, readjusted his collar. Then he noticed the hawk stooping above and smiled the sort of perfect smile which costs a fortune.

And Hart saw through that smile, down through his throat, past the man's cold heart and through the man's feet, down into the land beneath, the heart of the land, where fierce energies were shown, writhing like dragons and likely to cause endless trouble. And his own heart sank because he knew that the moment he had dreaded was about to come upon him, when the Merlin had to earn his keep as Merlins must, and the Arthur nowhere near ready to help him.

"Mr Vortig, somebody is sure to object," said the surveyor, but not forcefully because his salary was far larger than his principles.

The leader of the group, Carl Vortig, the pisser-on-sacred-stones, gave him a withering look. "Go quickly, and do what it is you have to do," he ordered, then raised his furled brolly like a rifle to shoot at the hawk, which soared away to that picnic on the distant hillside.

"Ambrose," he heard a woman's voice, his sister's voice: "Come back to us." The vision faded. He was back again, Yvonne's hand on his shoulder, almost tenderly.

"What?" she asked, and tapped his cheeks gently as he re-aligned his outer and inner vision, adjusted his time/space continuum as other men would fiddle with their zips before leaving the toilet.

"Go on sonny," he said, releasing the hawk and watching it soar off. It always made him feel a bit sick when he did that sort of spirit-travel thing: never had been a good flyer. The feel of the claws on his wrist lingered for a moment, and he rubbed the place.

"Ambrose, what…"

He took a deep breath, and sucked in his sister's cheap perfume which she bought from the local Pound Shop. Then he looked around, turning on his heels, as if he might never see the place again, and sighed.

"Time to start being ourselves, I suppose." And to Arthur, ruffling his hair without the slightest feeling of real affection: "Come on you little twat, let's get you home…"

Strathnaddair was, and is, a very real town. We have all been through it. It exists at that child-like level of consciousness that we can all access, if we can remember how. But we would have to remember the time on our mammy's knee when we sat and watched children's television, with the puppet characters driving through their puppet world, and us completely wrapped up in the doings of Postman Pat or Fireman Sam or Pugh, Pugh, Barney McGrew and the rest of them, while completely believing that when the screen blipped into nothingness their worlds still existed somewhere, and the characters acted out their dramas unceasing, never quite human but never wholly detached from humanity – and touching us all deeply.

Strathnaddair was real all right. The people died and bled. They had affairs, debts, loyalties and divisions. They suffered. They achieved. They had blocked drains. But if you looked at them with the soaring eye of the merlin there was also that in them which acted out endless scripts, and made them take on roles in a low-key cosmic drama that never stopped. All of us, in every town, slip into Strathnaddair's dimension from time to time. It is the kind of primal place: as it would be if the world were perfect, and seen through the eye of a child.

Not surprisingly, it needed someone to protect it. Which is why The Merlin of Strathnaddair just had to deal with the threat head on, and couldn't let it pass no matter how much he got his bollocks slapped along the way.

That was his job.

That is all of our jobs.

The great pile of Vor-Tech International towered before Hart and his dog like a cliff. All sharp and functional, chimneys like turrets, the vast walls covered in massive off-white tiles and broken by small blue framed windows, so it looked liked a cross between a medieval castle which had seen many onslaughts and an Atlantean temple from that sleazy period when they started cloning. Steams and vapours rose from the ground; dark clouds scudded past – or were they disrupted astral energies? Hart couldn't rightly tell, being too busy indulging in a last cigarette before breaching its defences, and trying not to meet the disapproving gaze of Shuck.

"Hey, yer just a dog, okay? What do you know about habits? Even the *greatest* Merlins have their wee vices. Ah look, we're not in Strathnaddair, we're in the Wastelands. I can have a good puff without worrying about the bloody ecosystem for once." He took a long final drag and held the smoke, drawing in his gut and puffing out his chest so that he had to hold his belt in case his jeans fell down, then blew the smoke out toward the dog, scornfully, like it was dragon's breath.

Shuck moved back and settled down, ignoring his master. If dogs could do 'disdainful', then Shuck did then.

And what song did Hart hear carried on the wind in this fell place, at this time? He inclined his head to one side and then the other; he looked up at the sky and pondered.

"*Ride of the Valkyries*, eh? Good one I suppose, though a bit too much bass at times. Ah well let's go kick yon Vortig's arse. Are you coming or not? No? Ah well you just sit there and do nowt as usual. *I'll be back*, as we terminators say."

If you had been one of the people sitting at the endless regimented rows of desks in the open plan offices, heads down and typing, with some of your brain cells dealing with columns of figures on your computer screen and the rest trying to scan and defragment your mortgage, you would have seen the great doors at the end of the large room burst open and an overweight ex-biker in jeans and leather jacket standing there with a certain magnificence.

"No' bad for an entry, eh ladies?" he said, almost strutting, hands in the pockets of his leather jacket, making it spread out like wings, proceeding down the aisle between the workers. "You probably think I'm Marlon Brando from *The Wild One* but no, it's only little me. My Hollywood days are *long* since over. Mind you, ye should have seen me at Agincourt. I was in me prime then, Miss Brodie!" – said with a wink at a spinsterish woman carrying toner cartridges.

The people stopped working. Their screen savers snapped into action and pipes, like serpents, started covering their work.

A small man with an ill-fitting hat and badge on his grey uniform which said 'John Horne, Security', tried to stop the intruder but kept bouncing off as Hart headed toward the double doors at the far end of the room.

"You see – sorry – but I'm not sure if it was Aldous Huxley or Jim Morrison who said: *'There is what you know, and what you don't know – and in between are the Doors…'*"

He clashed through the next set, revealing another long room behind, with more startled faces behind more desks. The young guard was powerless to stop him.

"On the other hand it could have been my Aunty Betty. Very learned woman she was. She put chunks of carrot in each ear to stop the, er, *voices* y'know."

He crashed through the next doors similarly, with yet another room full of secretaries and yet another set of doors at the far end. The guard continued to fuss and scurry like a gnat, his future depending on this confrontation with what he saw as a big lump of lard.

"Nice try laddie. Nice name too – Horne – one of the Old Names as we say."

"Out, you fat bastard, or —"

"You'd have liked my Aunt Betty. Timeless, she was. Her own voice was a cross between Winston Churchill and William of Normandy – although between ourselves she had considerably more facial hair than either."

At the final set of doors, the young and frantic guard dithered, dreading what lay beyond them. *A* young female secretary appeared.

"Hadn't you better call the *real* police?" she sneered.

"Ah leave him be, lass. And just remember: evil cannot create, but it *can* infect… *you* know what I mean, eh? Wink wink," he said, one eyebrow raised. She blushed as if he had touched a nerve.

At the final set of doors Hart was gentility itself, opening them carefully, as if the handles were delicate. On the other side, behind a large desk, Carl Vortig sat waiting.

Hart raised his arms like a downmarket messiah, smiling hugely, benignly.

"Lo," he said, "I have come among you bearing glad tidings of great joy! — or maybe I'm just here to slap your bollocks a wee bit."

"Who the fuck are you?"

You could have sworn that Hart liked this man. He was all warmth and recognition, as if they were the old friends who hadn't met since college days. "Ah come on Vorty... take away a few wormholes, morphic resonances, and Time/Space anomalies, you *know* who I am. Though I grant you, it's been a long time – if you look at time in linear terms."

Vortig looked at him, bewildered, strangely troubled, as if he almost understood.

"Look, if you want to sell me a *Big Issue* there are easier ways of doing it."

"I'm here for the biggest issue of all. I'm here to stop you building on the moor."

"How in the *hell* did you know that?" cried Vortig, leaping up and sending documents flying. Men and women appeared from nowhere to collect them, and restore them.

"A little bird told me."

"Get out of here... you know nothing! Security! Get someone in here now! Will someone rid me of this troublesome beast? Security!"

Hart leaned over the desk so that they were face to face. He could smell lightly-cooked mangetouts; Vortig could smell Woodbines. "I know everything, actually. I know that you plan to bury nuclear waste. I also know that if you do, the radioactivity will return to the surface in groundwater. It'll contaminate the land, rivers, and eventually the Irish Sea. The land there is unstable."

"Ooh I'm sore afraid! What are you anyway, a seismologist? Geologist? I've had the top men onto this. There's no danger."

"Then the top men are wrong. There is grave danger to the land and its people. You know, underneath the land," and he gestured with his hands, weaving them in and out, each finger almost taking on a snaky life, "there are energies which writhe, like dragons..."

"OUT!"

A sound of sirens. Vortig thought for a moment then head-butted his own desk, leaving an immediate bruise.

"Oh so over the top, Vorty. But impressive in its own way, I'll give you that much. You'll have me done for assault, right? Okay I'm going, I'm going..."

More security men arrived in blurs of grey uniforms. Hart shrugged and turned to leave. "I *have* to stop you. It's part of the Pattern. If you can just remember, you'll understand that. It's not personal." And then he added tartly: "Oh and by the way… the *feng-shui* in this place stinks!"

"I want him charged with assault," said Vortig coldly, pointing to his own forehead as two real policemen took over and hustled the intruder out. "Go in peace, brother. Or maybe just peace off!"

As they escorted him out he picked up a crystal vase with a single rose in it and did that strange thing with his mind which affected the material world in trivial ways, and gallantly gave an exact duplicate to the young secretary, the original staying where it was on Vortig's desk.

"Just try to remember *who* we are, and *what* we are, and *why* we are. You can't stop me…"

Vortig looked at the duplickated rose and the simpering girl, and sensed Hart's fondness for ladies. He stared at the crystal of the vase and seemed to see something within it, seemed to be thrown back toward something very odd, very old – if indeed you looked at it in linear terms. Perhaps he remembered something, some wisp which came from his own genetics and the dreamtime of his race. Or perhaps it was more a case of recognition than ancestral memory because Vortig knew in his heart that being a tyrant was like a tincture in the blood: all men had it in some way, to some degree. So had the fat git who had just greased into his office.

Hart's banter continued to echo back from the next room. Vortig blinked, rubbed his brow, stared into the fluted crystal again and put it down so sharply that it cracked.

"Door – lock!" he said in a certain tone, and the voice-activated mechanisms did exactly that. "Curtains – close!" And the long drapes slid across to cover the high windows. "Maybe I can't stop the bastard," he muttered, "but I think I know a woman who can. Phone – get me Vivienne…"

Vivienne lay in the sunken bath, in a room lit by stars beyond the glass roof. Candles floated on the surface of the waters and she made them move in elegant patterns by the idle motion of her thighs. If she had had a personality at all she could be said to be luxuriating, as if after a hard day. But Vivienne was more witch than woman: more purpose than person. When she wasn't fulfilling her mythic role as Seductress, taking on whatever elements of humanity were still left to her, she could almost be said to exist in this floating state, in this half-light, forever, like one of the cryogenic bodies that float in their tanks waiting for the day when science can rebuild their systems, and revive them. Like Strathnaddair itself, she exists within us too.

A telephone next to the bath rang. Her eyes opened slowly, strangely golden, like flowers at dawn, and her face turned to look at the art-deco piece which had disturbed her dreaming. One slim and elegant arm reached across and picked it up, her body making adjustments in the water to remain afloat. She listened. Words poured into her head like the current of a battery. She became more aware, alert, but without quite losing the languor. Anyone who didn't know magic might think she was well gone on smack.

"Hellooooooo..."

She listened and laughed, but very gently, very briefly, more a cough than anything truly jocular. "I knew you'd want me again... The same? Get him sorted? Oh how charming. Who is he? What does he look like?" The languid manner faded as she listened to Vortig's words. Suddenly galvanized, she sat up; candles were capsized and hissed their flames out, the wax making auguries. "I think we both know who he is... wake up, Carl, oh wake up and *enjoy*..."

She sank back down in the water with an almost blissful air, took a deep breath then submerged herself completely. Anyone watching might have been surprised at how long she stayed under. If anyone had cared for her – really cared instead of merely desired – they would have grown concerned, and made to stoop down and pull her from the depths. But after a timeless while – minutes, hours, days, months decades and aeons accumulating like dust – she suddenly rose, a naked lady surging splendidly from the lake, the languor replaced by a sharp intelligence which lay somewhere in that awkward cusp between sublime beauty and workable evil.

"'ere!" she said, trying on a Mockney accent, sorting out a role. "Yeah… cockney sparrer, that's me. Let's be 'avin ya! Toim gennl'men per-lease…!"

The regional police station. As he checked in with the Duty Sergeant, small elemental beings played around the desk, unseen by anyone else, taking advantage of the fact that the Merlin was preoccupied. They'd all rue if one of his gnomes got into the computer, or the undines messed with the water cooler. He snatched at one, then another, and put them in his pocket. Not that he actually did so literally, but the symbolic act had parallels in the occult worlds and so had the same effect, as any Merlin could tell you. But to the desk sergeant he was merely waving his arms about in a very strange way that probably spoke of too much cider.

"And now your occupation, sir?" asked the man behind the desk, well used to his sort and daydreaming about his own wife and why he wasn't getting any.

"I'm er… I'm a sort of speculator. I deal in Futures, as they say."

"So you're unemployed," he suggested, but he kept hearing his wife say that she didn't fancy *anyone*, not just him, it wasn't personal.

Slightly stung, Hart replied: "Well as a matter of fact, I'm a Merlin."

"Which means what, exactly?" – which almost certainly meant that she was humping Darrell at the Dairy, the Mr Wonderful who couldn't do a thing wrong whereas he couldn't do anything right.

"It means, officer, that I express and channel the dark, fecund brooding spirit of the land!"

The sergeant sighed a world-wearisome sigh and concentrated.

"Would this 'dark, fecund, brooding spirit of the land' be situated at 9 Orchard Street, Strathnaddair?"

"Aye, more or less…"

"Unemployed…" he wrote.

Now Ambrose Hart, who really *was* The Merlin of Strathnaddair, might have had eldritch powers of a certain and highly specialised kind, but he was also scared of being locked up, and there were very strict rules about how and when Merlins might use their powers for personal advantage.

"PC Scroop!" said the sergeant to the young constable watching the procedure. "Take his holiness to Cell 3."

The prisoner, who could intuit thoughts with reasonable accuracy, looked up sharply. "You know more than you know," he said cryptically to the man behind the desk, and added: "She hasn't; he would; she might; start talking."

"Just get him out of my sight," said the sergeant with great sadness, never realising that the insights and solution had been offered which could have changed everything. The moral being: be careful how you relate to the local wino or the village idiot; you might be talking to a Merlin.

Straightening his shoulders, Hart followed the young man who seemed as embarrassed by the situation as by his uniform, which was stiff with newness and obviously had never had its first vindaloo spewed down the front on a Saturday night.

"You look far too sensitive for this, sonny. Tell you what, I'll beat myself up. Won't take a minute. Cuts out the middle man. Saves police time and public money."

"In here please sir."

Hart went in and out.

"Have you got one with a better view? Ah well. It isn't your fault. I won't be making a complaint against you."

He looked around the cell; jokes came to his lips but failed. The young policeman hovered, something was on his mind. He peeked back outside to make sure no-one else was listening then said:

"You said you were *a* Merlin. *A* Merlin."

Hart picked up the accent and smiled.

"Oh, a Welshman eh? Ah, fey like all of them! You sense the strange electricities which rage through my veins, no doubt. One of my cousins came from Wales, poor sod. Did quite well for himself. He was a Merlin too, of course, though he did a bit of plumbing on the side. But listen sonny, not all of them cut the mustard, and at this moment in time, I am probably *The* Merlin."

Scroop blinked. He could have sworn he heard a sort of *Ta-Da!* played somewhere on tinny trumpets, and while he still registered that he wondered why the prisoner kept slapping himself around the hip and crotch.

"The Elementals, y'know. Can't live with 'em, and can't live without 'em. Not if you're a *real* Merlin that is. Quiet down in there lads!" he cried peering down the waist of his jeans. "Peace be still! That sorta thing."

"You're taking the piss."

"Oh I'm sorry son. Old habits. I've taken a lot of grief from your Welsh Merlins over the centuries."

"So have you got a weird and wonderful prophecy for me?"

"Prophecy? I haven't done that since I fainted on a grassy knoll in Dallas. Well do you want something cryptic, like the old one about the ass in the owl's nest on the walls of Holyrood? Or do you want the winner of the four-thirty at Haydock?"

"I don't understand a word you're saying…"

Hart looked weary. He looked old. This was one of the burdens of the Merlin: to be in the world but not of it; to get close but never comfortable; to see all things but never be understood or completely accepted.

"They never do, sonny. The best way for us Merlins to hide is by standing on a hill and telling the whole world, because the world doesn't understand, and won't see… but wait! Okay, I'll tell you something: You can only hold me here if you charge me. If you don't charge me, you have to let me go. So here is your prophecy: *You won't charge me. And you won't let me go.* There. And I will never darken your towels again."

The young man shook his head, bewildered.

"Look, erm, if you want anything, just call. I'll get you some food from the canteen."

He left, and as the cell door clanged shut in the way that all cell doors should, in an effectively repressive society, Ambrose Hart sank onto the hard bed and felt very very glum.

He couldn't judge the passing of time. Merlins are always rather hazy about such matters. But some period later he was still sitting on his bed, a tray at his feet and empty greasy plates. One of the gnomes was sliding back and forth across the grease as if it were an icy pond. Hart picked up a small plastic glass of water and duplickated it, then drank them both, trying to ignore the faces that peeped out of the walls, mocking him: old lags who had been there in the past, leaving the spirit of their moods like snot. He had many notions of Hell, of course, having been pretty damn friendly with Dante at one point, and this was certainly one of them. Other Merlins might have taken this in their stride, having other powers and working at different frequencies, but 'Strathnaddair' as his peers called him was about to scream.

"Time for a wee bit of self abuse," he said softly, nodding his head as if at some internal voice. He gestured to the elementals, two of which were perched on the frame of the door.

"Y'see guys, as my old pal Isaac Newton once said (rather pompously I thought), 'Matter can neither be created nor destroyed'. 'True enough Zac,' I told him, 'but did you never think it could be jiggled about a wee bit?' That's what us Merlins do, eh? So come on, do the business. Meld into the structure there and earn your keep. You know the sequence: gnomes of Earth, undines of Water, sylphs of Air and yon bloody salamanders of Fire… come on lads, chop chop!"

He stared hard at the door, ran his hands around the frame and then over the surface, breathing deeply, seeming to suck its essence into himself. And then, at the adjacent wall, he reversed the process, creating a duplicate cell door in the blank wall. He stood for moment, pleased with his magic, picked up a cold chip, ate it, then walked to the door and pulled it open, stepping through to find himself behind the counter of the canteen.

There were a few people in the canteen, but apart from the woman in the serving area no-one noticed the brief appearance of the cell door, or the man who stepped through it, looking rather anxious. He might have been The Merlin of Strathnaddair, but a small part of him was also Ambrose Hart, who had very human concerns about law and order, and not getting caught.

Before him was this small woman wearing the compulsory silly hat that all who worked with food were inflicted with. She looked at him open-mouthed, as if he were a salmonella virus on legs, and at the mystic door which now faded back into the wall. To his left was a sign marked EXIT.

"I'll just be er…" he muttered, pointing to the way out. He hated it when he was caught doing the magic. "Oh listen ma, I work undercover y'see. Camouflage. Now you see me now you don't. That's why… oh hell, is that the time?" He was about to escape through the doors when he was tapped on the shoulder, and almost cried out.

"They let you out then," said PC Scroop. "You were wrong about the prophecy."

Hart was nervous. He was not The Merlin in his power just then, just a very ordinary fella who wanted to go home.

"Not all wrong. A bit perhaps." He waved to the woman as he left, and she was still looking with open mouth at the space in the wall where he had appeared like some earthbound spirit. The younger man held both doors open for him.

"I'm not surprised you ended up in here. It's like a maze, this place. I'll show you out."

"Thanks pal," said Hart, in the fresh air at last, shaking the man's hand. "You'll be an Inspector one day, that I promise. Little pips on yer shoulder. I can see 'em. So mote it be."

If Strathnaddair exists in another realm, and yet is also a real place that we have all visited, then so are The Arthur, The Merlin and all the rest real people, with addresses, postcodes, mortgages, debts, and all the troubles and triumphs of modern life. You can find them in any phone book, just look under your own name. For there are moments when, if only for the blink of an eye and on the canvas behind its lid, we *become* them: for magical moments we become greater than human but often less than Good. A brief connection with another heart, or impact with another libido, and we can know ourselves as Sex Demons, Heroes, Champions or Damned. We can see as The Merlin sees, tempt as Vivienne tempts, and control as only Vortig can. We cannot do it successfully ourselves: we need another. With luck it is a lover who can empower and envision us, and make us sparkle amid the streets of Strathnaddair, and give us some quality sex along the way. More usually, dreadfully, fleetingly, embarrassingly and least effectively of all, it is our mothers.

So there was a crucial sort of day in Arthur's misfiring life when his mam gave him some spending money, straightened up his clothes, wet the corner of her hanky and wiped a stain from his cheek, then – with all her hopes resting on him that sometime soon he might become Someone – she sent him off to the Museum with all the other children from his year.

Strathnaddair's Museum was one of those Victorian places which were midway between a small Abbey and a Big Game Hunter's den, with stuffed animals littering the corridors, vast paintings of forgotten battles on the walls, and musty cases of dreary items that smelled like your maiden aunt's bedroom. Each child was armed with a clipboard and a sheet of questions that had to be answered, and were loosely shepherded by three harassed-looking teachers trying to maintain a reasonable balance between exercising firm control of the children and ripping open their throats. They were led by Miss Butler, a young woman whose life still curved like a question mark and who had just begun to realise that being made Head of Year was no compensation for the vigorous life she had left behind in the City to come here, which increasingly seemed like Nowhere at all. While in between the Kodiak bears and the Simpsons Gazelles, a young curator was looking at her with thoughts of doing some stuffing of his own.

"Right! Get into your groups!" she cried, and was a little astonished that they – more or less – did just that. She was an Outsider, still an unknown quantity. They were hedging their bets and – for the moment – allowing their human sides to prevail. "Or go around with a partner. Remember that we are searching for specific things relating to our past, which might tell us who we are and where we came from, with adequate clues given on your sheets. Answer all the questions and meet back here in one hour. And don't touch anything! Not anything!"

The children divided themselves accordingly into their mafia-like allegiances, until only Arthur was left, staring at the light refracting from some crystal ornaments in a case. A gaggle of girls near him saw his rapture and started to snigger, but one of them detached herself and came over.

"Hey, er, you boy!" cried Miss Butler, not sure of his name. "Wake up please! Haven't you got a partner?"

More sniggering. Who would partner *him*?

Arthur pulled his gaze away from the spume of light, the other dimensions that he glimpsed within the crystal. In the large hall of the museum, with its black and white tiled floor, he looked like the last pawn on a chess board.

"I'll join you," said the girl, and ignored her pals who were going *Ooooooh!* while wondering if they were missing something.

"Well thank you, Gwen. Now the rest of you… search high and search low. Three, Two, One… *Quest!*"

The children dispersed, in chaos, their voices echoing throughout the building. Some of the stuffed animals looked exceedingly worried.

"Nice lot," said the curator, sidling up to Miss Butler, looking her up and looking her down, and in his mind's eye using his tongue as he did so.

"Personally I feel they should have been held more as babies. Preferably underwater."

The old teachers' joke was lost on him. He was lost on her. She grabbed a small boy by the collar.

"Norbert…" she said menacingly, "that is a reproduction of the Venus de Milo. It is for the aesthetic delight and visual joy of those few souls in Strathnaddair blessed with a sense of culture. It is *not* for grubby little boys with far-away looks in their eyes to rub up against. Do – you – *understand?*"

Norbert, an unappealing boy with pebble-thick glasses, did strange things to readjust whatever was going on below his waist and ran away.

"You the, er, headmistress?" he asked, all his childhood traumas meeting and blending with his darkest fantasies.

Miss Butler looked around, harassed and annoyed and hating herself that she had given up her cosy world of Special Needs teaching for this. She had special needs of her own, and they weren't being met here. This, she promised herself, would be her last school outing. In future she would take up full contact karate or join a Japanese game show.

"I'm just a teacher," she muttered, walking on to try and shake him off, eyes on everyone but him.

"What do you teach?"

"I teach… *bastards!* Bruce! *Bruce!* That's a claymore not a pencil-sharpener!"

She pushed him aside and hurried off.

The children, meanwhile, mulled around the exhibits, arguing in their groups, while Arthur Cornwall and Gwen Fisher stood awkwardly together before a glass case containing items which told the fascinating story of Strathnaddair's history as a town where cider was made. At least, Gwen stood awkwardly. Arthur sort of flickered where he stood, like a living flame. It was quite beautiful if you liked eerie – which she did. The boy avoided any eye contact with her to the same extent that Miss Butler had done with the curator, but in his case it was an expression of his autism rather than distaste for courtship rituals. Anyone who knew him – and few did – would have told you that he was extremely aware of the girl who peeped at him from behind the safety of the clipboard.

"You're new," he said, his gaze fixed on the early cider mugs once owned by the Mathers family known to all at the time as the Cider Kings because they made and drank so much of it.

"No, I'm the same age as you!" she said brightly, but saw from his frown that he didn't understand this sort of thing. Unlike the curator, who could just about qualify as an Earthling, his lack of understanding was all to do with what they all called his 'condition', which was something that Gwen seemed to sense, for she was old, very old, as some children are, and wasn't even into lip-gloss any more as all the others were.

"It's a joke," she said, but kindly. "*You* said —"

"Hey dickhead!" a voice roared across the room. It was Cooky, the school bully, a podgy young boy who had entered puberty long before the rest of them and constantly whipped it out to prove it. "Come and see this! It's a painting of yer fat git uncle!"

The teachers went over to do some crowd control, but were intrigued also. When Gwen and Arthur got to the fringe of the group they were allowed to the front and found themselves staring up at a large reproduction of a 14th Century painting which showed Stonehenge being built by Merlin. *Original in the British Museum*, said the hand-written legend beneath. And there, putting final touches to a trilithon, was Merlin, who was identical to Ambrose Hart. Or put another way (for they are both the same) there was Ambrose Hart fiddling about with Stonehenge – and he was the spitting image of Merlin.

If Arthur rarely made eye contact with his peers he looked with some intensity at the painting, and Gwen took full advantage of this to stare at him.

"Don't be upset," she soothed, touching his arm while the rough boys jeered and sneered, taking their lead from Cooky.

"I'm not. That's him. That *is* my uncle. He is a big fat git."

They look at the painting again, together. Then Gwen looked even harder at her partner, and it was as though light shone through him like it had the crystal in the case, and she realised that he was probably the most beautiful boy on the entire planet in the whole history of the world.

Back in his small house, Hart carefully stacked some tarot cards in a form reminiscent of the Stonehenge trilithons. The room was, as ever, full of Elementals busy at different tasks. He cajoled them like the school teacher at the museum.

"Aye, just remember, the gnomes deal with the solids, the undines the liquids, sylphs all the gases – no smiling please sylphs! – and you salamanders sort out the radiations. And lets have no mixing the elements. Remember what happened when the Jehovah's Witnesses visited!"

He straightened up his collection of videos, featuring his favourite actors: John Candy, John Goodman, Sydney Greenstreet, Orson Welles, Oliver Hardy, Roscoe Arbuckle, Wallace Beery, Robert Morley, Burl Ives, Alfred Hitchcock, W.C. Fields, and Charles Laughton… fat bastards all. "Hi guys!" he said cheerily enough, and answered himself in some of their voices, so it was like Hollywood in his sitting room for a minute.

Hart, you see, liked his voices. He could do them all, and did. He had only to hear someone speak once and he could repeat it, note perfect. When he was posing (which was often) he did all the Big Ones – the stars of television and screen that everyone could recognise; but he was also constantly slipping into the Little Ones that only he knew – transient voices from forgotten programmes he had heard as a boy, or from neighbours long since passed over, thus preserving his own past in tiny ways, and creating jokes known only to himself. Whether he was hiding, or expressing the Everyman that all Merlins should, was a moot point between him and his sister. The Jehovah's Witnesses who wangled entry once, and overheard this, told him that – like Satan – his name was Legion; and although that hurt him a bit he could see their point as he booted their arses down the garden path.

Really, he had to get out more.

Then, as he always did whether it was necessary or not, he walked over to kiss a framed photograph of a nun that hung on the wall. "Hi Mam!" he said, then nodded to the spirit creatures, adding: "My bark is worse than my bite. Isn't it Shuck!"

The dog looked the other way.

He heard the clatter of milk on the doorstep, went to bring it in. Outside, everything was lush, clean, verdant and peaceful. Birds and sunshine. Nature spirits were everywhere in his garden. He paused and looked around, self-satisfied.

"And Merlin is on his hill, and all is well in the world…" but was vaguely irritated by the way his underpants had disappeared up his backside, and needed some jiggling to get comfortable again.

And as he turned back inside he didn't notice the small cloud which briefly covered the sun, although Shuck briefly came to his feet and looked behind his master, as if there were someone following him.

As before, one pint of milk was turned into two. He put the original in the fridge and poured himself a glass from the other. The phone rang. He went back to a sitting room which was full of otherworldly creatures, scuttling like mice: Elementals, tiny dragons, mysterious spirit-lights which winked and bobbed. Had they been material, he might have called in the pest control man. He settled into the couch, turned to the sporting pages of the newspaper and pressed the loudspeaker of the phone.

"The Mystic Brotherhood awaits your request," said Hart, using one of his many voices. "Please state clearly where you saw the advert and whether you need to speak to a Yogi Master, Wiccan High Priest, Urban Shaman, Celebrity Clairvoyant, or any of the other occult authorities we have here."

Even Merlins have to earn their keep.

There was a long pause and then a timorous female voice sort of sneaked into the room. "Well, I do a bit of yoga, so I'd like to speak to a Yoga M-master, please."

Hart never faltered, just reached for a pen and ticked off something in the newspaper. "He may be busy with his kundalini now – tricky thing, the serpent power – but I'll try and connect you…"

A click of the remote control and mantric chants began, fading away while he turned the pages to the football section.

"Om Shantih Om! Sri Mahananda here," he said in his cod-Indian, fading the chanting to a background drone. "I expected you for to call. As I am sitting here in the full lotus, or padmasana as we supple fellows are calling it, I am feeling your presence in my third chakra…"

He started doing a crossword, feet up on the coffee table.

"Oh wow, ahm, well… you see I've got an interview today. Just a j-job-share at the cider company. I'm a single parent you see. I really need the job. I do a bit of yoga – just the half-lotus, not like you, but I wondered if I – if I could have some chant, or something, to g-get my confidence up beforehand. Things are a bit tight and…"

Oh bollocks! he thought. Even Merlins earning their keep can feel guilty. Especially those who remember that their brief is for the Common Man, whom they should never betray. He sat up, throwing the paper and pen to one side and interrupted:

"Perhaps you are more being in need of my excellent clairvoyant friend in the next lodge. He is being an old chela of mine. I will be putting you through. *Om Hari Om!*"

He made an appropriate noise then played something Noel Cowardy, the voice changing to the plummy tones of High England.

"Simon the Celebwity Seer, here. *Jolly* nice to empath with you. Now I understand that you are *weally* anxious about an employment opportunity?

"Oh I am, yes!"

"Hmm, well, I can assure you that on the hour you *will* be confident, you *will* make a good impwession, you will *not* be cursed with that blush, or be twoubled by mysterious feminine pwoblems on the day, and you *will* get the post… You *will* get it. Do you hear me, dahling? Twust me. You. Will. Get. It." Whatever personality he had, he forced down the phone line with all his might and main, and you could just feel the change in the woman's tone.

"Oh I do trust you! I *do*! Hey I'll call you afterward, honest! Oh… thank you so much. You don't know how —"

"All wight dahling, all wight…"

"Oh I'm sorry sir, sorry. Now… how do I pay you?"

"No need," he said softly. "Have a *splendid* day!" He hung up, sighed, closed his eyes and muttered in his world-weary way: "So mote it be, eh?"

He toyed with a cigarette, fighting the urge to light it. One of the salamanders ran up his arm and tried to do so, to tempt him, but he flicked it away.

"Right," he said, putting the newspaper in the rack and taking the empty glass to the kitchen, "now to sort out that Vortig…"

The doorbell rang. It cost him 99 pence from the Pound Shop and played 12 very tinny different and generally unrecognisable tunes, and he loved things like this because he had the impeccable bad taste of the Everyman. He frowned, not expecting anyone.

He angled his mind in that direction because Merlins can usually get some sense as to what lies behind your average door. Muttering, he went to answer it, flinging it open with some ire.

"If it's the Holy Grail you're after I —"

He caught his breath. A small tremor – perhaps not measurable on the Richter scale but powerful nonetheless – made him tremble from the calves, right up to around his knees. There was Vivienne, looking lost on the doorstep with two suitcases and a standing, salon-type hair dryer, a tight blue cotton dress which kept very close to her slim, *somebody-please-touch-me* figure, and the sort of ruffled hair which spoke of great but helpable distress.

"I… I er… One moment, Miss!" he slammed the door shut and sank back against it, looking with horror at his untidy house. He took a deep breath. "Right" he said briskly, loud enough to command but not loud enough for Vivienne to hear. "I want the gnomes to do the floors, the undines to wipe the windows and polish anything polishable… Then I want the sylphs to give us nice breezes – er, lemon-scented I think, with a hint of somewhere Mediterranean." The curtains twitched, he sniffed the air and nodded. "And the salamanders – oh hell, do what you want, just don't leave burn marks on the furniture."

The creatures burst into action; within seconds the house looked immaculate. Hart nodded approvingly and opened the door again, giving an apologetic look. Vivienne was still there on the doorstep, looking bewildered. Almost like a backdrop, crows made a racket like football hooligans in the trees beyond his garden, but he never listened to *that* musick.

"Sorry about that! The dog, he – er…"

She smiled. He had never seen a face shine like it. His heart was pounding. His mother had warned him about this sort of thing.

"Hi! You must be Mr 'art. I've come about yer empty room."

Hart, who could do any voice, and collected regional accents like records, knew that this one came from a far-off land indeed, in a world that was almost light-years distant from his own: Penge, probably, or maybe even Dagenham. But he was still bewildered by the sense of her words as much as her accent.

"The empty room…? This was the real secret of the Holy of Holies, y'know – that it was in fact *empty*. Is that the one you mean?" He was burbling; he blushed.

Vivienne frowned. The sun went in. "The one to let. Here. 'Share bathroom, toilet and large sitting room.' That's what I was told."

"Y-You must be mistaken…" he said, and he could have ripped out his own tongue and stamped on it because she looked so crestfallen.

"But I was told… a woman in the salon said. *That's all right darlin'* she said, *Just turn up* she said."

"A woman?"

"Some mouthy old slapper with her roots showin'."

"Ah, you've met my sister! But she didn't tell me."

There was a pause. Neither spoke. Both looked at each other. It was the girl who broke the silence.

"Oh gawd," she sighed, dragging her hand through her own golden hair and making it more bedraggled, her features more distraught, and so desirable that he didn't know if this was love at first sight or an actual heart attack. "I'm sorry, Mister 'art. I feel a right fool I really do. Sorry to trouble you."

She struggled with the hair-dryer and cases, and turned to go, making an awkward and pathetic way down the path, wobbling slightly on her high heels. He was completely besotted of course – which man with a pulse wouldn't be? – and it had taken about 3 nanoseconds if measured in that linear way which caused many of his problems in life. He found himself rushing forward, never having broken into a run since his early thirties, all apologetic, no longer just a fat old git but suddenly a knight errant who had a chance to rescue a reasonably distressed damsel.

"Wait! It *must* have been sis. She's always trying to… Well, there *is* a room, and I *do* need a lodger. Just leave all this here, come in and talk terms."

She looked around anxiously. "Someone'll nick it."

"Hah! Not from here. Not from *my* property. 'Believe what I say' he declaimed, copying Jeff Bridges in the film *Star Man*, though no-one on this planet would know that. "Oh please, come on in."

He looked up and down the idyllic but empty street, almost guiltily, and gave a silent *Yes!* to the ever-disdainful dog.

Inside, Hart was nervous as a schoolboy. He made her tea, chattering inanely but also nodding thanks to the Elementals who had tidied the house so well.

Vivienne was looking at the photo of the nun, sweating after her walk in the hot sun, flicking her dress off her body to get some cool, exposing tantalising glimpses of flesh.

"Are you a Catholic then?" she asked.

"Me? *Me!* Oh that. That's my mum. Yes. Yes. She was a nun. My father – ha ha! – well he was – if you believe the Mother Superior that is – the Prince of Darkness. As if the Prince of Darkness could work on the cold meat counter at the Co-op, that is. Sugar?"

"Three."

"Same as me!"

If ever he wanted an omen it was then, and all his teachings about them went out the window: *When you see an Omen, it is **always** a bad omen. Then when you see an obviously **bad** omen, it's even worse. Always.*

Unthinking, he duplickated the cup of coffee and handed it to her, keeping the other for himself. She looked astonished. It took a second before he understood why. Flustered, he walked away. Merlins were not supposed to reveal themselves. It was almost drilled into his DNA that: *No true Merlin ever calls himself a Merlin. And you should play pocket billiards rather than show your hands weaving light and darkness.*

He opened the door of the spare room and gestured inside. He hoped his gut wouldn't block the doorway, and so sucked it in, thrusting his chest out massively. She slid past, and he felt the nipple of a firm, pointed breast rake against his shirt like a questing finger, and his legs almost gave way.

"Overlooking the garden. Nice room. On a clear day you can see the Eildon Hills."

He tried to centre a glass ornament on the windowsill but in his nervousness he made another duplicate. In a slight panic by this time he hurried back out into the sitting room, and Vivienne followed, astonished.

"What did you just do? 'Ere c'mon!"

"Nothing! What do you mean? Nothing!"

"Hey listen… if I'm gonna be your lodger – and I'd really really *really* like to be – we gotta be honest. Always. The one thing I like about a fella, more than looks, more than money, is his honesty. I've had enough of blokes lyin' to me. So tell me… I didn't imagine that, did I?"

Hart hung his head as if in shame, but in truth more in a state of hopeful embarrassment. "No you didn't," he confessed. "Sorry. I don't get many visitors. Specially not…"

His words tailed off, he couldn't look into that perfect face in case he drowned, coz he knew that all the undines in the universe wouldn't be able to save him from those depths. Vivienne lifted his head with her hands, very gently.

"My oh my, that's the loneliest face I've ever seen… but tell me. How?"

He stood up straight, pushed his shoulders back. He could have sworn he heard Aaron Copeland's *Fanfare for the Common Man* trumpeting in the aethers.

"Because I'm… because…" he sighed, struggling to say this out loud to a complete stranger. "Because I'm not *really* a fat bastard, I'm really a series of a series of pulsating geometric patterns, if only you knew how to look properly. And I'm more than that, much more than that: I'm… I'm the Merlin of Strathnaddair."

He looked at her expecting the laugh, the sneer, the taunt; there was none.

"Well bugger me," she said, astonished, sitting down sharply on his couch.

While Ambrose Hart was, in his own unpractised way, preparing the ground for the sort of love rituals and magic that he, as a Merlin, had never experienced, Vortig was out on the moors. This was not a place that the Best Dressed Man in Britain liked being.

"What is it about the Scotch and their heather?" he moaned, stepping around another clump as he watched the heavy plant equipment manoeuvring into place, their yellow metal bodies lurching and turning like dinosaurs in a mating dance. The land was torn up; birds flew their nests; small animals scurried to safety. Dead animals littered the ground. As a committed vegetarian, he didn't like such mess.

"We'll never get away with this," said a Politician, anxiously but not too stridently because he was well inside Vortig's pocket.

"We can't afford not to," said the latter, very calm and casual, summoning a drink from his voice-activated chauffeur. "*You* can't afford not to."

"What about that lunatic Hart? What if he gets this in the papers, or to the Cabinet, or Greenpeace?"

"I think our friend Hart will have his horns pulled soon."

"I don't want more violence! Please."

Vortig looked hurt. He almost seemed vulnerable. "Why use violence? I abhor it! There are far more powerful energies we can use."

"If the people find out…"

"The people… oh bless them! Soon, they'll see Vor-Tech as their saviour, the only way out of the hole." He held his arms out in Saviour fashion, almost wishing he had some stigmata on his wrists, threw back his head and closed his eyes, breathing in the country air.

"Always smells like shit in the countryside," he mused, as something akin to a Thunder Lizard roared past.

At the same moment, back in Strathnaddair, light streamed into the spare room. Vivienne and Hart were face to face and he was trembling into love. Of course he never stood a chance. For years he had been exceedingly wary of women, and had generally found by limited personal experience but much observation of others that, as a species, they set out to change their men. Then, when they succeed, they don't like them anymore. With all the wisdom of The Merlin he had always vowed never to let that happen to himself – which was probably why he was a lonely fat bastard who hadn't had anything in decades. So now, facing this creature of delight and firm pointy breasts, he knew that she could make him into anything she wanted.

"You've, er, you've lost an earring," he said, all his Voices gone.

She reached and touched the bare ear.

"Here," he offered, using his odd magic to create another one identical.

If Vivienne could do perms and the very latest styles, she could also do awe, and she did that now, and it crept across her perfect features like the dawn. "You *are* Merlin…!"

He started to relax.

"Actually I am *a* Merlin, or even *the* Merlin. It's a title, you know. Every community, every Age has one. Though I have to say there have been Merlins, and then there have been… *Merlins!* Believe me, it's true."

As he said that, the heavy drilling equipment took the first deep bite into the land, while Vortig looked happily on. Hart frowned: he had just felt the tremor of this. He might have done something but Vivienne gently touched his face and turned his head, as if in wonder, but really to keep him distracted.

"Oh I *believe* you! All my life, since I was a little girl, I've dreamed about meeting someone like you. Dreamed about meeting Merlin – I mean, sorry, *The* Merlin. I knew you existed."

Hart swallowed hard. Very hard. "Did you indeed?" he asked feebly.

"Was that magic with the earring hard to do? Could you teach me? Nah, I don't suppose you could."

"Oh I could teach you anything!" he said, pitifully eager. "That with the earring is easy. The presence of crystal, quartz, silicone makes it a doddle – although, as we say, 'Nothing comes from Nothing'. Oh yes, I could teach you…"

"Everything?" she asked, coming nearer, putting a hand on his chest.

"Everything. Well, except – traditionally – for one little spell of no consequence."

"Which is?"

"Ah, the old one entitled 'How to trap a man without walls or bars'. Useful in the pre-feminist eras I suppose, but not something that *we'll* be needing, eh?"

She changed her tone. Her voice lost its cockney-sparrer shrillness, became soft. "I bet some women find you irresistible. I bet some of them can see through to the *real* you…"

Hart swallowed again. In the silence of the room it sounded like a breeze block hitting the floor.

"Well, the feral qualities of the *true* Merlin – especially the *Scottish* Merlin – *are* said to be strangely attractive…"

He reached toward her. She moved out of his reach, lithe and quick as one of the Elementals. Back on the moor a digger pushed against the first and largest of the stones in the old circle. At that precise moment Hart blinked, took a sharp breath, and might have 'seen' the desecration but Vivienne undid her suitcase so that it burst open and her delicious and varied underwear spread at his feet. And she was blushing like a virgin, and he was breathing heavily, and the sovereignty of the Land was the *last* thing on The Merlin's mind just then.

Of course nothing happened: the art of the temptress is to suggest availability without ever making it easy. They had an evening of manners. Light chat. Pizza and a video of *The Fisher King*, and Hart amused her with his voices. He had never met anyone who had found him so funny before. Usually he began to irritate after the third impersonation, and by the fifth they were making their exit. But there she stayed, feet up on the coffee table, slouched on the sofa next to him, looking at him with doe eyes and rapt attention. *Oh you are so funny* she kept saying, and he began to believe that this was the woman of his dreams – or rather, the woman he wanted to dream. At last, a woman with the strange power of being able to see through the blubber of the Fat Bastard and marvel at the Adonis beneath.

"Most women think I'm a big slob," he confessed, like a shy little boy.

"I like what's in 'ere," she said, tapping his heart, which almost burst.

At bed time they said Nuh-night like shy children, and closed the doors of their adjoining rooms almost in unison, and he didn't get much sleep coz the Moody Blues in his soul played *Nights in White Satin* relentlessly, though he didn't mind at all, what with him being used to nylon all his life.

The next day, a perfect day, they walked in the countryside around Strathnaddair. He wanted to show her his territory, doing a sort of 'beating of the bounds' as they used to do in parish churches.

She walked rather awkwardly because of her heeled shoes, which kept sinking into the grass. He could do many things as a Merlin, but his powers couldn't stretch to solving that problem. So when she reached and took his hand, as if for support, he almost gasped. Her hand was tiny and cool, and felt – oddly – like the dry coolness of a snake. But he wasn't complaining.

They walked on. She kicked off her shoes but didn't let go of his hand. Inside his head The King was singing: *Take my hand, take my whole life too...*

"Right you. Now... you gotta tell me everythin', young man. Warts an' all." She squeezed his hand as she said that. Amazing the things that can be read into a simple act of pressure. He took a deep breath.

"*Are you sitting comfortably? Then I'll begin,*" he said, using a voice from *Watch with Mother*, then realised that this kiddies telly programme had ended many years before she was born. Yet she never blinked. Then in a normal and slightly contrite tone he really did begin, and it felt like therapy to explain himself for once.

"It's hereditary, being a Merlin. Usually skips a generation. Same with The Arthur, and The Morgana – they're titles too."

"Are there more Merlins?"

"The Merlin is… well, legion. Although some don't quite 'cut the mustard' as we say. In fact, there's a Merlin down in Orpington who is causing us all some grave concern…"

"You said you'd teach me," she said. In fact she said it so artlessly that anyone with half a brain cell still functioning might have seen through the words to her ulterior motive. But when you're a Merlin you can have all the wisdom of the magi and still not be able to understand women, iron shirts on both their collar and cuffs, or form an effective relationship.

"Easy as…" and he snapped his finger, whereon a small rainbow sprang up, and she gasped.

"Oh I ain't clever enough. Not me!"

He stopped, put his hand gently on her shoulder, felt ecstatic that she seemed to enjoy his touch, and made no attempt to pull away. Why is it that handsome men can put consoling and innocent hands on a woman's shoulder without complaint, but when a fat git does so it constitutes a grope?

"Viv, 'clever' is the worst thing you can be. All you have to do is suspend disbelief, act 'as if', and let other powers help. Set yourself free, inside."

Above them, a hawk stooping again.

"Ah we've got mail," said he, summoning the bird as before, borrowing Vivienne's silk scarf to wrap around, doing a sort of Ta Da! when it landed on his wrist. Vivienne shrilled with delight. He was about to look into its eyes for a message but she was so excited – leaping up and down in a girly way – that he turned his face to hers, and the creature took fright, crying out and flying off again. Hart hadn't seen the death-look that she had given the bird, which the bird knew only too well. So she stopped it telling him about the desecrations out on the moors. He was bewildered and might have tried to call it back but she stroked his brow and he stopped worrying after that. And in fact he could hardly walk.

"I want the hawk to come to me," she pouted.

Hart smiled paternally. "Ah no, you have to find your own totem. Mine just happens to be the hawk – or the *merlin*, rather. *Falco columbarius* to give it the proper name." He hoped the little sod Arthur had got his facts right.

They walked on. The hills were around them. The day glistened. The breeze sighed in the trees. She took his hand more surely in hers.

"That trick you do, where you make copies of things. Can all the Merlins do it?"

"Oh no no no! That's *my* speciality. We all have the broad spectrum of magical talents, based upon the senses, but we also have our own little tricks. One Merlin is briefed with talent for making 'Light things Dark and Dark things Light' – whatever use is that eh? Another can 'Turn the outside in and the inside out'. Who knows what he can make of that, eh, except when taking things out of the tumble dryer. Honestly… some of them are just carried, if you ask me. But I, the mighty Merlin of Strathnaddair have the talent for 'Duplickation' as I call it – with a *kay*. I gave Madame Blavatsky some entry-level lessons in the art, so she could impress dear old Colonel Olcott. She duplickated small items of office equipment: pencils, coins, throwing knives… but that's about all. Duplickation… it's not a great word but I can't think of a better one, can you?"

"But *how?*"

"Floating about in the atmosphere are particles of every visible thing, but in a highly diffused state. By an act of will, and visualisation, I can form these into more or less any shape that I choose. It is question of – well, *visualising* things; it is based upon the sense of… touch."

He looked at her meaningfully, trying to be suggestive and what he imagined to be sensual at the same time, which to an objective observer might have invoked imagery of rhinos charging at Land Rovers.

"Oh wow…" and she did a wonderful show of a young woman with very little brainpower going to the edge of overload. "Hey I been into some pretty weird things in my time, like rolfing and pitta bread, but this…"

Hart expanded his chest, and his voice. "It's a talent that's not without precedent, however. I read somewhere about a fella who used it to feed five thousand people with cod and chips twice. Although personally I think that's a wee bit OTT, eh?"

She looked blank. He loved her even more. He flipped a coin; when he caught it, there were two coins.

"I want that power, Ambrose. I'm not joking."

She used his name! The woman he loved had used his name!

"Please," she gasped, her head tilted slightly to one side like a little bird's, eyes pleading. "Teach me a little something now. Now. Oh please. Please please *puh-lease*…"

They were skirting dense woodland. Hart stopped and turned her to look into it, standing behind with his hands on her shoulders, trying not to be stunned by the electricity which flowed from her body to his, or the bum like a peach, or the smell of a perfume which made him want to eat her.

"Look…" he said, pointing to the woods. "Look into the darkness between the trees, into the ancient forest from where all things sprang…"

Vivienne looked, she leaned back against him. He tried not to swoon, marvelling that she had a unique power of her own: of being able to turn the mighty Merlin of Strathnaddair into a Big Girl's Blouse which flapped helpless in the breeze, all its buttons undone.

"Now, er, act *as if*… as if you're the most magical creature ever to swim out of a man's dreams. *As if* you have power to enchant all the creatures on this planet. *As if* you're more than a little hairdresser from Penge, but a portion of the sun at dawn…"

Ooh she said, and he didn't know if it was because of what was rising behind her, or what was emerging from the forest, and to be honest he didn't care.

Slowly, nervously, a stag came from the darkness between the trees and paced toward her. Vivienne gasped, but Hart held her steady. He was good at that, he suddenly realised.

"It's your creature. Your totem. Be still…"

The stag bowed before her. "Touch it," whispered Hart, and she did, gently, and it rose, turned, and went off into the darkness again.

They stood for a long moment. Even a biased outsider might have agreed that Vivienne seemed genuinely moved by the encounter.

"I'll tell you what," she said, turning to flick her fingers through the mop of hair.

"What?" he asked, hardly daring to imagine.

"Why don't we go back to my… bedroom. I'll give this… a bloody good seeing to. It's… very long."

"Please," he gasped. "Oh please do. I can't do a thing with it. The salamanders, y'see. Awkward little sods."

"I've got some ideas. Then I give you a good blow … dry. Afterwards."

Hart made a strange whimpering noise in the back of his throat, and nodded.

Vortig lay on the therapist's table, on his stomach, with a row of acupuncture needles stuck in his back with a handsome woman named Vestigia manipulating these in turn, like joysticks. Her long black hair, streaked with flashes of grey, was tucked into the collar of her white coat. There were men in suits in the background, looking on.

"You see, Innes, it was Carl Jung – a relative of mine – who once said that 'Everything happening at a given moment of time has qualities inherent to that moment'. Do you follow?" They nodded, lying, but he knew that. Although he didn't have Hart's powers of far seeing, he knew that at that very moment there were bulldozers approaching the old stone circle and ceremonial avenue on the moors with instructions to level everything. It wasn't clairvoyance, just a simple matter of schedule. "Well anyway, you're sure it's all going ahead."

"It is, and very fast too. I just worry about the local authorities and public opinion."

"I told you, they are well taken care of. But you're sure – *sure* – that the land is stable enough. I can cope with the old farts of Westminster and Strathnaddair – I don't want Washington and Moscow on my back."

"It's stable!" said the Advisor in genuine surprise, wishing the woman would do his own meridians for him. "Who told you otherwise?"

Vortig frowned; an image of that clown Hart swam into view. He shook his head, gasping with relief as the woman jiggled another needle.

"One thing though. The remains of the old stone circle and its avenues…"

"They'll be ripped up. Believe me, no-one will fight for *them*. What use are they anyway?"

The men filed out. He groaned with pleasure as Vestigia sank another needle into a crucial meridian.

Gwen and her mother Elaine waited at a bus-stop near the T-junction which formed the centre of the town. Gwen was at the age when it was just *so* embarrassing to be seen with her mother, and kept a marked distance away so that anyone looking might think them complete strangers. When she had to talk she did so out the corner of her mouth, making no eye-contact and not speaking a decibel louder than she had to, praying all the while for the bus to hurry up.

The stop itself was set in a sort of hollow, with one short and steep arm of the T stretching off uphill to their right, shops at either side; the other to their left sloping more gently, curving over the small river; the third and central arm straight ahead of them, through a very narrow canyon of houses, leading up the steepest hill of all.

Here in the centre of the tau-cross, where they waited patiently, exhaust fumes made her cough as a new convoy of lorries squeezed past, making the buildings shake and the glass in the shop windows quiver. Gwen pulled her sweater up over her nose; at her age she could still do that. Her mother was oblivious to the traffic pollution, being too busy looking at the jobs section in a local paper, wrestling the large sheets and trying not to elbow the passers-by on the narrow pavement.

Now Elaine was one of those earnest but insufferably nice women who had little personality of her own but instead filled herself out with New Agey beliefs, and dallied with the idea of becoming a Wiccan. She adorned herself with crystal pendants and power bracelets, and a brooch like a Native American dream-catcher until she could decide for sure which path to follow, hoping to catch whatever energies might be drifting past her soul in the meantime. She wasn't even remotely aware of the large man ambling past carrying flowers, half-humming and singing *Maria* from *West Side Story*, but with the name adapted to Vivienne.

"'And *sud*-denly the world will *nev*-er be the same again! *Viv-i-enne hmm hmm hmm hmm hmm…*' Oh I'm sorry miss," he concluded, as he bashed against her arm and she lost her grip of the paper. There was some mutual fumbling, the situation was restored, smiles were exchanged.

"Have a good morning!" she told him, as he went on his way.

"I will. And it *is* a good morning. It's a *splendid* morning!" and you can guess what had happened to *him* last night.

Elaine looked sharply as he spoke and sauntered off, crossing the road and heading off up the hill. She was sure that she recognised the voice. And so she had, for she had been the anxious lady who had called him about the job interview.

It was Gwen who spoke first. "That's Arthur Cornwall's uncle. It has to be."

"Why's that?"

"I saw him in a painting."

"What painting, mm?"

"In the museum. It was 400 years old."

"Hmm," said Elaine, who as a single and lonely parent had got into the habit of scrutinising every male which came near, and had often found them wanting. Wanting a shag, most of them. In truth, she wasn't into sex, much. Or rather she hadn't let much sex inside her. Gwen was the result of a single quickie with a travelling folk-singer who looked like Bob Dylan, sounded like Donovan, and wooed her with a song about a boy with a moon and star on his head, by Cat Stevens; and after the third spliff he had had her all ways up and round the block, never to be seen again. She never felt entirely comfortable with men her own age, and likely to be thought of as potential mates. She preferred being with older people, ancients, so the Sex Question (as she charmingly thought of it) never had a chance to arise. She was capable of Love, certainly and truly, but ached with knuckle-biting frustration that it had to include so much physiology.

"He doesn't look a day over… over… well, not *that* much."

Hart was too enraptured by his memories of the previous night to be aware that two young women from different generations were staring at his back. He was still quivering from the first kiss, the first touch, the warmth and the glistening that he had known with Vivienne. That, and all the other things that would fill the mind of a fat git who had just been laid by a perfect young woman who – against all logic – had thought him wonderful, and showed her own wonders again and again.

At last, he could be himself, and be loved for it. No longer did he have to worry about his looks, his waistline, his greying hair. Vivienne had shown him that these things did not matter, that she could see something special within, and that she was not shallow like the other girls. Bliss was it in that dawn to be alive, but for a Merlin t'were very heaven!

"'I'm Free!' he sang, from the rock opera *Tommy*. "Duh duh duh, duhduh, duh duh duh *duh!*"

He did a soft-shoe shuffle past two mothers with babies in their prams, who stood gossiping, almost blocking the pavement.

He smiled at the babies, feeling the benevolence that only those in love can know.

And then his smile went.

Merlins might have many obscure and possibly useless talents, but sometimes they can also *know* things. He looked at the babies and then up the empty road which rose sharply and curved behind some tall and old buildings. He could see nothing, he could hear nothing. At least not on any human levels.

"Ladies… would you move, please?" he said to the young mums, very earnest and urgent.

The two women adopted attitudes and postures of disbelief and irritation. They knew *his* sort.

"Lissen pal, we're no' blocking anybody's path."

It's not that —"

"Ah clear off you fat old git!"

The fat old git, deeply troubled, looked up the still quiet road. There was nothing to be seen, yet he knew it was coming: the old tractor, pulling an overloaded trailer. Behind him, Gwen and Elaine were looking on, aware of the altercation but too far away to hear exactly what was being said.

"Please… if you'd all move along the pavement, just a few feet – oh please…"

"Sod off! Clear off you old poof!"

And then it was on them, like a beast, all red and roaring, its lights blazing and apparently coming straight at them, the load of hay wobbling. In desperation he grabbed the handles of both prams and pushed them in parallel, roaring: "Move out the bloody way!"

The mothers, not realising the danger he had foreseen, only saw their children being snatched. They screamed and ran after him, pulling at him, tearing at his pony-tail, kicking the backs of his legs, but still he pushed the prams. It was then, as the tractor turned into the main street, that its load finally became unbalanced and toppled off the trailer, crashing onto the spot where the mothers had been standing with their babies, demolishing the adjacent wall.

Babies cried, dust rose, the tractor driver looked ashen, hay drifted down like snow, the wheels of the upended trailer

46

spun like roulette, and people came from the shops to see the devastation. The mothers had stopped in mid-blow and looked at the wall, and then at their babies, and then at Hart with a confused blend of wonder, apology, thanks and shame.

Embarrassed, relieved, and making sure that they all saw him limping heavily, he retrieved his flowers and walked on, only resuming his jaunty step when he had turned out of sight.

"Who *was* that man?" he said proudly to himself, using the voice that everyone used when they had just seen the Lone Ranger ride off into the sunset.

"*Who* did you say he was?" asked Elaine, back at the bus stop.

Even the greatest cosmic dramas need mundane locations to give them credibility. Here in Strathnaddair the location happened to be the Co-op. Ambrose and Vivienne were pushing a trolley together, giggling like children. She had done his hair, so it looked like early Elvis; he was wearing a new leather jacket, new boots, and his best jeans, with a sort of bootlace necktie. Viv took down a packet of 3 condoms and looked suggestively. 'Brose, as she called him, raised his eyebrows in sequence, looked both ways and then up to make sure it wouldn't be caught on camera, then 'duplickated' them into a dozen packets.

"I lurv the smell of sex in the morning," he said, doing his Robert Duvall from *Apocalypse Now*. "It smells like… napalm!"

"Ooh you do make I laugh," she laughed, but quite genuinely. If a man can't inspire lust in a woman then laughter is the next best thing.

Then as they turned the corner of the aisle they bumped into another cart, being pushed by Yvonne. She looked frostily at them both. And when Yvonne did 'frosty' you have to think in terms of permafrost, heading toward Absolute Zero.

"No, don't tell me, I never forget a face…"

"Ah come on sis, I meant to call around. I've been busy."

"So I can see," she said, looking into his cart. "This is your *Vivienne*, then?" she asked, and you could almost see the italics in the way she said it.

Hart turned and put his arm around the girl, who smiled sweetly at him and his sister.

"Hmm, you've got an awful lot of live yoghurt in there sis! You wanna let the air get to it."

"Bastard."

"Bitch."

You could tell they loved each other.

"Anyway that's Strathnaddair for you. A man can't fart without the whole town knowing."

"But that's the point of the Merlin, isn't it?" said Vivienne coyly, and seemed unaware of The Look that Yvonne gave her brother.

"Listen sis, she er, well, she knows everything. She's an enchantress in her own right. Descended from Mother Shipton, I think. She's read all my bumps. I'm just honing her natural skills."

"I bet he's given you a right good honing, hasn't he?"

"Actually 'Von, we watched a video. We needed our tissues didn't we 'Brose, eh?"

"What – you showed her one of your pervy ones!"

"Ah sis! It was *Brief Encounter* actually. It was *sad.* Not… we didn't…"

Vivienne sensed the friction; her face became serious. "Look I'll er, go and pay for this and leave you to talk. I'll see you outside. Nice to meet you, Yvonne."

Yvonne gave her a frosty smile, and Hart a shy wave, doing the silly thing with his cowboy necktie that Olly Hardy used to do.

Brother and sister watched the young woman as she paid at the check-out. She looked oddly vulnerable as she filled the carrier bags, and certainly blushed as she hurriedly scooped the condoms out of sight.

"Well?" asked Hart. "You look like you swallowed a wasp."

"She. Is. So—"

"What?"

"Gorgeous. Bloody gorgeous. Even I could fancy her. I'm pleased for you Ambrose."

"Liar!"

"No I am, really! It's just…"

"Just that I'm a fat slob and she's like a goddess."

"No! Well I mean —"

"Listen… Inside every fat bastard is an enchanter wildly signalling to be let out. She can see the *real* me."

"No it's coz you've never had a proper girlfriend before. I was starting to despair."

"Well *excuuuuse* me! This coming from someone who's never been with a carbon-based life-form in many a long year. Anyway… anyway what about the sublimely sensual Sian? We were an item. We'd have got married but for a technicality."

"Ambrose, she tried to get you certified."

"Yeah, well that was the technicality. But… but what about the lithe and lissom Lorraine?"

"The one that ate your tortoise?"

"Aye, well… but it was a mangy wee thing anyway. The divine and dainty Daphne then! She was crazy about me. Had everything a man could want…"

"Yeah yeah yeah … big shoulders, moustache. Ambrose she joined the Gurkhas!"

"It was the Royal Horse Artillery, actually."

He looked at Vivienne, framed in the doorway, limned by sunlight.

"I've got to make this work, sis. I'll never meet anyone like this again."

He walked toward her with a cheery wave, giving a knowing wink to the local yobs who were leering at her and assessing their chances.

Not a chance, laddies! he said to them, mind to mind – if they had minds. They looked at her and they looked at him, and he knew what they were thinking – insofar as knuckle-draggers like them could think. He burst into the old party song, dancing toward his woman, taunting them: *I ate all the pies, I ate all the pies… This fat bastard, this fat bastard, I ate all the pies…* He had a girlfriend at last – a real goer – and he wanted the world to see. There was nothing like blowing his own strumpet.

Yvonne, who had known as much frustration in her own life as her brother, and who could tell exactly what was going to happen without needing any powers of clairvoyance, sighed deeply.

"You big soft bastard…"

They were sitting on the couch, preening each other like two apes: adjusting an errant hair here, a displaced whisker there. The phone rang and Hart was about to reach over and pick it up but Vivienne pressed the loudspeaking button.

"Hi," came a woman's voice from afar.

Hart, somewhat embarrassed, replied with: "The Mystic Brotherhood is closed for contemplation at the moment. Please leave a message after the tone. *Beeeeeep…*"

"Oh, er hi again. Hi… I want to contact Simon the Seer. Tell him… tell him I got the job. Mind you I was made redundant the next day but no-one could have foreseen that."

Hart looked guilty. He wanted to speak but held back. The woman continued:

"I'm not complaining! Simon gave me confidence I'd forgotten I had. He really did me good. I almost felt his presence at the interview, helping me. Tell him I'll speak to him again, sometime, and to thank him for giving me hope. I'm going to try for a place at Vor-Tech next. Bye."

The Merlin of Strathnaddair frowned. *Vor-Tech…* He might have exercised his memory then, instead of his glands for once, but Vivienne sat astride him, brushed back his hair, and Vor-Tech was pushed into another dimension.

"Why d'ya do that? When you were at the shops yesterday you 'ad loads of calls for this Mystic Brotherhood thingy. Why?"

"Because there's a need. It's what they want. It's my job. The Merlin has to make an honest living. I give them good value, within the rules."

"You could be a billionaiiiiire."

"Oh could I, Nurse Ratchet? I told you, Nothing comes from Nothing. There is a price for everything, and everything must balance. The Merlin cannot profit from his people."

"You sound like a right pompous twat when you talk like that."

"Pompous! Moi?" He took up the newspaper and looked at the racing page. "Just in time – strangely enough, eh? Haydock 3.30. Montmorency 30/1 outsider. That's the winner."

He picked up the phone. Dialled. "Ken, it's me. Aye. Okay okay. Do me a favour pal will you, and put £20 on Montmorency in the 3.30 will you? Yeah yeah yeah she's here now, I can't talk. Okay, ta." Then to Vivienne, as he reached for the telly's remote control: "He wants to know if you're a natural blonde. This bloody town…"

But his face was glowing with pride. In fact it did more than glow, it was like the Chernobyl reactor, he was so made up coz the whole town knew that he – the Fat Git of Strathnaddair – was doing the business with a sex goddess.

Vivienne was very quiet, deeply intrigued. They sat on the edge of the couch and watched the race, getting more and more excited, starting to scream as the commentator screamed then jumping up and down with delight when Montmorency came in first.

"How much? How much?"

"£620," said Hart, suddenly calm and serious, walking to the door. The letter box opened. A brown envelope was pushed through. Hart caught it before it hit the floor.

"Oh," he said in mock surprise. "It's from my dear friends at the Inland Revenue! Oh goodness gracious me… it's a tax demand! Here, Viv, read it. Tell me how much they want from me in back tax…"

"£621," she said weakly and wonderingly.

"Quod Erat Demonstrandum. Which means, roughly translated, *The Merlin never gets owt for nowt*."

"Who taught you all this?"

"My master, Blaise. Although I called him Wolfy behind his back, because that's what 'blaise' means, in the old tongue.

What a lad I was, eh? Here's a picture..." He rummaged through a drawer and pulled out a sketch of a grey-haired man with a double-pronged wand.

"That's him, though he can take any form he wants, really. The Merlin of Limpley Stoke told me that *his* teacher had spent the better part of ten years in the shape of a tea cosy. You can imagine the fun they had on an evening, eh?"

"When were you taught? Recently?"

"Well, ah, the Merlins are taught at the onset of puberty when, er..." he mimed the dropping of his balls. "There are tremendous reserves of energy floating around at that time, you see. Especially with me!"

The house shook as a convoy of heavy vehicles bearing the Vor-Tech logo thundered by outside. Hart was about to look but Vivienne grabbed him.

"Where's your master now?" she asked, very close, grabbing where he had just mimed.

"Who knows? At this moment, who cares?"

"Then be my master. Teach me. I want it. I want it all..."

Grrrrrrrrrrr......

The memories of Hart's courtship clustered like a bunch of flowers, lightly held by a red ribbon: he would remember the first time he duplickated a flower for her, and the rapture on her face as she tried – unsuccessfully – to do the same for him. He would recall summoning small creatures from the garden – shrews, moles, squirrels, field mice – and how she squealed with delight when they assembled before her. And best of all was the time when he touched her on the brow and gave the power to see the world as he saw it, with its Elementals, its tree spirits, Ancestors, wild faery beings, earthbound souls, forgotten gods and goddesses all lurking in another dimension which intermingles ours, and seeming to focus on his house in particular, so she found herself living in a storybook where fantastical life-forms were part of her own existence.

Once, he started to show her the future in a pond, but as the picture built up he would have caught glimpses of machines on the moor if she hadn't thrown in a stone to distract him.

Oh how they laughed.

"Could you walk on water? Could you raise the dead?"

"I'm only the Merlin, I'm not…"

"Come on sweety, don't be modest! This little mouse…"

A field mouse had come to her hand. She put out her palm and it climbed on. She lifted it up tenderly, gently – that's what he loved about her. And then she broke its neck.

"*Viv!*"

"Then save it," she said, and he saw another Vivienne then. "Use your magic. Teach me how."

He took the little body and put it down, scooping a hole in the ground, not able to look at her face.

"There was no need for that."

"Then bring it back. Bring it back I said!"

"I can't. It's an old rule: 'Only a life can pay for a life'. Honestly Viv, I'm a wee bit disappointed in you."

"Listen, it was gonna to die soon anyway. I was kind and quick. Hey look!"

She pointed to a hawk stooping, then pulled him to her and kissed him, tongue down the throat, hands all over him. Any man would have forgiven anything for that. Mollified, the idyll resumed. She was probably right: *It was gonna die soon anyway.*

"Oh come on you big wonderful beastie… do something else. If you loved me, you'd do something else. Something *new*."

Hart thought. He sensed. Then he stamped the ground. A mole rose to the surface and then sank back again. He reached into the hole and pulled a face; he pulled several faces. They ranged from simple puzzlement, increased bewilderment, mild surprise and then outright astonishment. "Behold!" he cried, and pulled out an ancient bracelet, all silvery loops and set with black stones, the sort of thing that would give men with metal detectors heart attacks. Viv put it on, and she was pleased. Oh she was *well* pleased.

"Thanks pal," said Hart, calling down the hole. "I owe you one."

"And I'll give you one" said Vivienne to the Merlin.

It might have a whole summer, or a decade, or perhaps a large portion of a Crowleyan aeon, but those memories were endless, eternal, as all memories of love are. And when she managed to duplickate a small goblet that he had made by wrapping silver paper from a Kit-Kat around his thumb, well that was the very best – and the very worst.

Act 'as if' he told her, and she had a natural talent, she really did. Plus she was backed up by the vast and radiating love of The Merlin who stood behind her, acting like a generator, making her hair stand on end. *What, all of them?* he asked once, leering.

She made rainbows, charmed the birds and beasts – with the possible exception of Shuck who was clearly a one-man dog and kept well out of the way when the magic was happening. She duplickated things with greater and greater skill, learning all sorts about mass, displacement, and balances.

"But be discreet, Viv. Discretion is the first thing that all must learn on the magical path. A fat git like me can *talk* all I like – no-one will listen. But the great unwashed mustn't actually *see*, coz that's when the trouble starts. The Merlin uses Mystery as one of his sources of power. The Merlin must live among the people as one of them."

"I don't like it when yer pompous. I like it when yer a bit thick. *Sssssssshhhhhh!*"

Then came the time when even he had to admit that she had it all, that her schooldays were at an end. It was late at night, under a full moon, sitting facing each other across the kitchen table which had seen a lot of action recently, and not all of it culinary. He duplickated a wine glass; she matched it. He duplickated a fork; she did the same. Cup, saucer, knife, napkin, spoon, egg-timer, salt and pepper shakers which looked like little yeomen, cracked plate, bent spoon, ancient breadboard... faster and faster, he could hear *The Hall of the Mountain King* being played in the aether.

"Anything you can do, I can do… *better!*"

"You can do anything better than me," he admitted, almost ruefully. "I'm impressed."

"Yes. You are."

"Come 'ere, wench," he said, in the mock manfulness which they had used to preface their sex.

"Get stuffed," she said in a soft but steely voice, and he was sure the temperature in the room dropped by several degrees.

When she turned her back on him and went off to their bedroom, loudly locking the door, he sat there for a long time before shrugging and whispering to the dog: "Time of the month, eh? Women eh? Eh?"

He found himself watching her. Watching her as Shuck often watched him, these days, so that he felt a bit of a dog himself, in more ways than one. There were things he wanted to say, things to ask, but he was afraid of the answer. Oh he could deal with hauntings and possessions, and evil spirits and creatures who had wandered into our dimension by mistake and needed a wee bit of guidance before they did any damage … but he couldn't deal with this small blonde woman drying her hair at the dressing table, with a fluffy pink towel around her perfect body.

He summoned up his courage, gestured to the Elementals to keep out of the way for once, and said: "Tell me. Do you still love me?"

"Still love you?" she asked, but it needed a lot of imagination on his part to hear the surprised tone and the question mark at the end of her sentence.

"Do you love me?"

"Yes I love you. Of course I love you," she said coolly, turning up the power on her hair dryer, brushing carefully.

"But really Viv. Do you *really* love me? How *much* do you love me?"

"Gawd you sound like a little boy. You sound as if you're the one 'aving doubts."

"*Me?* Me having doubts?" His mood suddenly soared. She had clearly been testing him in that cunning way that women apparently had. Well, he would rise to *any* test.

"Then show me. Show your love for me. Show me what your love is like."

He didn't need to think about it much. It had been in his head, and in his heart, ever since she had arrived on his doorstep. He stood up, shook his arms and flexed his shoulders and neck, preparing himself.

"Right. *Right.* You want a sign. A romantic, beautiful sign. I will *surround* you with my love. Eat your heart out Interflora…"

It was as if the whole room dissolved into the mist, with only her glowing at the centre of it. Then the mist began to disperse and Vivienne found herself surrounded by flowers of every shade and colour. She stood, and was ankle-deep in rose petals. Over her head was an archway of roses and beautiful medieval music played as a young deer walked up to her. Two white doves cooed in the greenery. She was dressed like some pre-Raphaelite princess, and the world of mortals no longer existed. She gasped, looked around her, and laughed – somewhat cruelly.

"Oh you old romantic, you! Now show me 'ow *I* feel. Yeah, c'mon, show my love for you. You can do that. You *are* a Merlin – possibly *The* Merlin. Go on, big boy…"

He loved it when she called him that.

"I can't do that. I don't want to be in your head, that would be wrong. I want you to tell me. Otherwise it would be an invasion, a rape, for me to steal your inner secrets."

Vivienne seemed genuinely amazed.

"You mean you *can*? You mean you can read my every thought but *don't*?"

"Yes."

Although he didn't notice, some of the flowers wilted at that moment as a fragment of her true self showed through.

"Hey, you can. You got my permission. Get inside my head. Show *my* love for *you*. Show *exactly* how much I feel. *Become* the love I feel."

What could he do? If Yvonne, or any woman with the tiniest remnant of moral scruple had been there, they would have warned him to back off and start running. They would have seen right through the little minx. But when you're an Enchanter trapped inside a fat git, you will take any love, no matter how treacherous, and accept any passion, no matter how false, than go through life knowing nothing of either.

"If you say so…" he replied, trustingly.

He shut his eyes, clearly expecting some display of massive sexual desire and passion. He held his arms up and … nothing happened. He shivered. Could feel the room darken. When he opened them he found himself sitting alone on a fallen tree in a bleak, wintry forest. It was snowing. There was no warmth or shelter anywhere. Just two massive blue moons which rose in the black sky and then sank from sight. And he realised where he was, what he was: a little figure in an ornamental glass dome. To be shaken for the snowstorm. Tacky as hell.

Vivienne smiled as she held the toy level with her deep blue eyes. She was fully dressed now, in the sort of clothes that might have graced some top toff totty in Paris or London, leaving the hairdresser's rags on the bed, and ready to go. Carefully, with a last remnant of the humanity she had only temporarily adopted, she placed it carefully on the dressing table in front of the mirror.

"Now I've got your very last secret: 'How to trap a man without walls or bars' she said, mimicking his brogue. "Wasn't so hard, was it?"

She looked at him for a moment, and there was almost sadness in her face. With a turn of her heel she was out of the house, kicking Shuck on the way, and climbing into the large black car which waited outside.

Anyone who stood outside Hart's house, in the little garden, would have heard and never forgotten the great cry of pain from the little glass dome within, the infamous *cri de Merlin* which all mortals know too, when they've been dumped, and which makes you sick inside and feel like you've been stabbed and then abandoned on an ice-floe, and which went something like:

NOOOOOOOOOOOOOOO!

Arthur and his mum walked toward the school, he some distance ahead, mind in another place, walking in a way that was almost a dance, his eyes on distant stars, his feet avoiding the dog-turds which littered the pavements now like Scud missiles. Yvonne and Ambrose called it his 'faery dance' – not that it meant gay, or wimpy, but because it resembled the odd lilting movements of certain spirits that lived in certain places. There was one which lived at the bottom of Miss Varden's garden which contorted itself quite shamefully if you'd had the sight to see – which fortunately she didn't.

The community was showing the first signs of decay: paving stones tilted, windows broken, tyres slashed. The greenery was not quite so green. Heavy plant equipment roared through the streets. A gang of boys appeared and blocked Arthur's path. He was aware, but seemed unmoved, looked everywhere but at them. The others didn't know if it was courage or stupidity. They might have done something. Their leader, the bullet-headed creature named Cooky put his finger up to Arthur's face as if he was about to jab him in the eye.

"Oh shit!" he said instead, when Yvonne caught up and glared. They scattered. In that part of the world, at that time and probably for all time, they were all scared of their womenfolk and had heard their dads and grandads mutter about the malign powers of the menstruating female, and all agreed there was no power on earth greater or more terrible than The Mam.

"Snot-nosed little gob-shites," she said, watching them go. She grabbed Arthur firmly by the shoulder. No good being gentle, or concerned, because he never liked being touched (it was an aspect of his autism, apparently) and you had to grab the little sod if you wanted to make contact.

"Are you being bullied at school? Are you?"

He twirled away, pivoting as if he had a different centre of gravity to everyone else, giving his gait a sort of marionette-like quality. "No. Not me. No."

"Are you afraid of them? Coz if you are I can —"

"No. Not me."

"You don't say much."

They walked on and stop at Hart's gate.

"Do you want me to go the rest of the way with you?"

"No."

He walked off. Cement lorries thundered past, throwing up clouds of dust. She watched him go, clearly worried as only mams can be. Not that she relished the role of The Mam. The truth was, even when she was a bit of an Enchantress herself, she never yearned, as many women do, to bear someone strong sons and become an Earth Mother type surrounded by her children's children and lots of Lego. The truth was, her own libido was almost entirely directed at her own sex, even though her brother – despite his awesome insights – had not the slightest inkling of that fact. She kept it well suppressed, she did. Even from herself at times. It had been her duty to bear The Arthur, and with the help of her brother's shape-shifting she had managed to do the business with a likely sire. But the truth was, she fancied Vivienne every bit as much as Hart did – as every man did – and so could see right through her.

Yvonne sighed a very lonely sigh, looked at the glowering sky and shivered, then entered the front garden. The gate creaked and scraped on the path, as it hung slightly off its hinges. It had never done that before. She paused at the front door and fingered the dying bushes and the hanging basket which had once been so lush but now looked like an old wig hanging there. There was an air of decrepitude about the once-immaculate garden. Frowning, she knocked on the door coz she loathed the tunes from the stupid bell.

"Jesus!" she cried when she saw the pathetic creature who opened the door, fully dressed but wrapped in a blanket.

"No, it's only your brother," he said in a small voice.

"Ambrose! What's happened to you?"

His face was grey, his hair was lank and uncombed. He had never shaved in days, and he looked as if he had never slept either. He tried to say more but the words failed – which, for a Merlin, is a serious affliction indeed. Weakly he beckoned her in.

She shivered. "Bloody hell it's cold in here! What's ha—" then she realised. "The little cow's dumped you."

"It's a mistake. She'll be back."

"What *has* she done?"

"Look around…"

Yvonne saw nothing much different at first, but then Hart put his hand on her brow, one foot on her foot, transferring energies, and then she 'saw' the whole atmosphere, and felt as if the whole house was a block of icy crystal, and her brother trapped inside.

"Ah you daft sod…" She touched his cheek. It felt frozen, the skin drawn taught.

"There's worse…"

He poured a coffee, which looked right enough, steaming handsomely. "Taste it." She did so. Nothing wrong with that. Then he duplickated it, and gave the second cup to her. Which looked like the first, steaming away.

"Looks all right to me."

"Put your finger in it."

She did so. "It's cold. It's steaming yet it's cold!" She sipped. "And its tasteless!"

Hart shivered. He pulled another blanket around himself. "I can still duplickate but it all goes wrong. Look…."

He took a flower from a vase, did his special thing: the duplickated flower was dead. He picked up a magazine, made another, then flicked the pages to show that they were upside down.

"I suppose I could work for the Guardian…"

Then he took his favourite photograph of Vivienne and duplickated this too. The copy was a sneering version of her.

"Well *that's* not so wrong!"

"Ah sis, she loved me. She told me so."

"Ambrose… I regularly tell you that you're a frigging idiot, but I don't…"

Hart took down the picture of their mother, the nun. He duplickated it. The copy was of their mother as a Page 3 pin-up. Embarrassed, he put it behind the couch.

"Forget her."

"Okay. Forget who?"

"Ambrose!"

"How can I? Eh? Look at me, the Fat Git of Strathnaddair; and her, the sort of woman a bishop would kick his stained glass windows in for! She was the greatest thing I've ever known. Or ever will know. Beauty. Lust. Look…"

He made his sister 'see' again, through his eyes. In the angular facets of the huge crystal in which he now lived there were myriad stunning images of Vivienne at her best. The purest object of his deepest desire. "That's what crystals do," he added glumly.

"Come home with me."

"I can't. I can't leave the house. No, I mean literally. I've tried. Watch…" He opened the door. To his vision the doorframe was sealed by crystal. He could not walk through it. He pushed, shoulder-charged, and kicked the barrier, but it was unyielding. "I'm trapped in this crystal cave. But she must want to keep me for something. I know she'll come back."

Yvonne shook her head. To her it was an empty door. She walked through it and turned, reaching her hand back across the threshold to her wreck of a brother. From his point of view he saw Yvonne's muzzy figure pushing her hand through solid crystal and beckoning to him. He touched it, and to his astonishment found himself yanked through to the outside world.

"Sis!" he said with genuine awe.

"The little tart didn't know *everything*. And you'd better call that mangy dog of yours, too."

He felt like a prisoner who has spent years in a small cell. It took him a conscious effort to make more than a dozen steps. Although he still felt deathly cold, he could – with the sour warmth of his sister – function a little better. Then when he looked around he almost wished he had still been trapped in his crystal cave.

"It looks like shite," he said, looking around his town, knowing it was all his fault.

"It looks like you."

"I'm no longer channelling the life-force. It's all going bad."

"But you're out now."

"Only because you got me out. Inside here…" and he tapped his heart, "I'm still…"

"You can stay out."

He looked back through the still open door of his house, into the crystal. He saw images of Vivienne, beckoning.

"I can't. Not for long. I can't come and go on my own impulse. I *know* it."

"Aye, well you're the Merlin. You know these things. I suppose I'd better stock you up with some TV dinners till you can get this sorted. And you're coming with me to parents' evening at the school, broken heart or no."

"Me?"

"Well if you hadn't —"

"Don't start! Not now. Okay, if you can get me out, I'll come."

She kissed him, tenderly, on the cheek. To her it was like putting her lips on a dead cod. To him, it didn't remotely compare with Vivienne's kisses. He watched her go and stared at the lorries thundering past, some of them with radiation warning signs on their sides. He called after her before going back into the crystalline house:

"Better get me a dozen pot noodles as well!"

Meanwhile, in Vortig's mock-Tudor mansion, Hart's obscure and mysterious object of desire was sprawled on a low red exercise bench in the very private gym, while Vortig exercised.

"There were times when I thought was the only real person in the whole town," she mused, the cockney sparrer act long gone.

He didn't listen. He was doing great things with weights and pulleys, exercising muscles in sequence as others might walk their dogs, so that his body glistened with sweat.

"Did you know, Vivienne – actually you won't – that our sense of smell determines whether and how we choose our mates? One sniff and your own DNA can communicate with someone else's, and futures can be chanced. What about my sweat? Would I make a good mate, dearest? A good sire? Would you bear me strong sons on the basis of these glistening drops in my armpits?"

She ignored him, picked up a small device for measuring blood-pressure and fiddled with the buttons. Her legs were sprawled obscenely as she lay on her back, her head dangling off the end; she held the object above her face to study it.

"He was quite nice, really. I've had worse."

Vortig stood up and walked over to the gymnastic rings which dangled from the ceiling. Drying his hands on a towel and then rubbing powder into them he leaped up and did several brisk twists and turns, finally finishing with his legs together, his arms wide apart bearing his whole body weight, all his upper-body muscles quivering and twitching.

"Do you like my six-pack?" he asked, using enormous self-control to make it sound calm and unstrained.

"He was *fun*. He made me laugh," she mused, and duplickated the device.

Vortig collapsed, plummeted to the floor, but said nothing. It disturbed him greatly to see that, and he didn't want to see it repeated. It was like someone who was squeamish about the act of childbirth: he knew it was fundamental, knew the broad and disgusting details in a fuzzy sort of way, but just didn't want to *see* it. So he pretended it hadn't happened. Otherwise doors that he had long since sealed might be forced open.

"Oh don't get sentimental! Did you stop him, that's all I want to know."

"Yes," she said in an almost wistful voice. "I stopped him."

Vortig did a series of backward somersaults all down the gym.

63

Hart had a sort of primal fear of going back to school even though the focus was on his nephew. He, Yvonne and Arthur sat on small chairs at the back of a small hall, waiting their turn while the teacher, Miss Butler, finished speaking to two distressed parents before them. Last rays of the sun streamed through the high windows. A large and very old clock ticked on the wall behind them. The whole place smelled of pine furniture polish.

"God you look rough," said Yvonne to her brother, out of the corner of her mouth.

"You're no sae bad yourself."

"I wasn't getting at you, I was just—"

The other couple got up to go. The woman carried on talking just a while longer. You didn't need the powers of a Merlin to hear her husband thinking: *SHUT UP SHUT UP SHUT UP!* At last they clumped out of the hall, their steps sounding very loud and echoey on the bare floorboards.

"Thank you so much for coming in!" the teacher called with only a trace of exhaustion in her voice. "I'm sorry that we're running so late. Mr and Mrs Cornwall isn't it?"

"*I'm* Mrs Cornwall. This is Arthur's uncle."

The teacher was embarrassed. Hart didn't twig why at first, then he leaned over.

"No, I really am his uncle. I'm her brother, not her fancy man."

Flustered, the teacher extended a hand, muttered about still being quite new. They took it and shook it. *Cold fish* thought Yvonne, who had certain powers of psychometry and felt that she could know things from a handshake. But her brother was reminded of Vivienne again, and his mind drifted back to the freezing crystal cave that had once been a cosy little house. *Ow!* he thought, as Yvonne kicked at his ankle. Arthur wandered off to stare out of the window, his forehead flat against the glass, rolling slightly back and forward.

"Arthur…" she said, putting on her glasses and buying herself some time as she pretended to study his report. "A very unusual little boy."

Yvonne gave a weak smile. She might have a tongue like a viper when she was on the street, but school and their teachers troubled her too.

"Well… your Arthur is a well behaved and quiet boy. He sets an example to others – and believe me in this school they need it. The other children think the world of him. No really they do! Well, some of them. He seems like a little adult, sometimes. But… nothing seems to interest him much."

"That's coz he suffers from what you lot describe as *autistic spectrum disorder*."

"Don't start," Yvonne warned her brother.

"He's got no friends," the teacher continued, "does not play with the other children, and his progress is below expectation."

"Well, I wouldn't go so —"

"On the other hand he's a genius at dates and calendars. Draws in a strange and beautiful way. Although he is clearly literate to a high degree, he looks at books rather than reads them – as far as you can tell – but sometimes startles you with his knowledge."

"Autistic spectrum disorder my arse. You only use the word autism coz you don't know what else to call him. You've seen my letters on the subject?"

She looked through the file, opened a long letter, remembered the correspondence.

"Yes, I remember it now. Sorry. I did reply. I must say you do write a vigorous letter Mr Hart. But I must ask – what about these odd additions. NW. BTW. PR."

"Obvious, surely! No? Note Well instead of that stupid *Nota Bene*. By The Way instead of *Post Script*. Please Reply instead of that ridiculous *Repondez S'il Vous Plait*. I believe in speaking plainly."

"My brother also believes that decimal coinage is just a flash in the pan, and that the 24 hour clock is likely to be a passing phase."

"Yvonne…"

"Ambrose…"

"Did you never think, Miss Butler, that my beloved nephew might just be a wee bit special, a wee bit different? That he might be in a different place to the rest of us?" He picked up a pencil from the desk and duplickated it, unconsciously, but the teacher didn't notice, she was reeling back from his onslaught. He flung the copy down in disgust; it rolled to the edge and the young woman stopped it, struggling to find the words.

"Look, Mizz Cornwall, although we have always tried to adopt the policy of mainstreaming all children with special educational needs, we have been looking at the possibility – just a possibility mind you – of finding a specialist centre for Arthur, and one which —"

"*No!*" cried mother and uncle in unison, and if they had powers of stopping speech then they did so now, because the young teacher could only open and close her mouth, no sounds coming out, and some awareness in the primitive centres of her brain that this was not the sort of *No* that ordinary parents might utter.

"You can speak," said Hart after a little while, and she swallowed and picked up the duff pencil, and hummed and hah-ed as women of a certain class do, and eventually said:

"Well, perhaps we might look at some form of one-to-one private tuition. Certain learning and behavioural disorders have proved to be immensely receptive to this sort of input." She tried to make notes, but the pencil wouldn't work; she was too nervous to see that it was made of solid steel, and could have acted as a bradawl.

"His uncle will do that," said Yvonne with a look that was almost triumphal. "Won't he?"

The uncle nodded. He had said his bit and was now doing what he did all the time these days: daydreaming about Vivienne. About the way she looked, and talked, and smelled, and felt, and touched, and those perfect pointy breasts. Those best of all. In his memory at least, she was thoroughly and completely duplickated.

"We have tried to find something to catch his imagination, something he could really get involved in, and he has shown some aptitude on the computer. I've been wondering about that. But it is so difficult to fit them all in. Thirty-six children, one computer…"

Hart became suddenly animated. He half turned in his chair to look at said computer, and as he did so Yvonne kicked him hard on the leg. He turned his cry of pain into a cough.

"Yes, we've found that children with au— I mean children with Arthur's skills and approach to life can often take to these. I think it's because they can learn at their own pace, and not be harassed by us, and can get sort of sucked into the learning aspects. Do you have one at home?"

"We'll get one."

Hart got up to inspect the machine.

"That one is so old," said the teacher. "It doesn't even have USB ports."

"No USB ports? Really? Ah the poor wee bairns! Shocking, simply shocking."

"Ignore my brother. He's stuck in the past."

"Okay okay… I'm sorry." He fiddled with it while Yvonne and Miss Butler sank into discussions about plans of action, and strategies, and support, and other things which bored him silly.

During all of this Arthur remained looking out of the window, doing that thing with his forehead, rolling it from side to side as if trying to smooth out the skin, or maybe just soaking up the light.

"Thank you so much for coming," the teacher said at last. "I'm sorry that we were running so late. You do know that my door is always open. I'm happy to talk about my pupils at any time."

"Arthur is a *very* special boy, you know," said Hart in a tone that was both insistent and yet apologetic for his own bullishness.

"Yes indeed. I have nineteen very special boys in my class."

"Aye, of course you do. Of course."

In the corridor outside, when she made sure no-one was listening, Yvonne said:

"You duplickated that computer."

"I did! And I put a wee spell over it so that it won't be noticed till Monday, and someone will wonder why it's not on the inventory."

"But will it work? What's the use of a dud?"

"Look, if it doesn't work then they can just take the dud one back to the shop; the shop will check the number on it, assume it's genuine; then the school will claim it off the insurance or guarantee; then they'll get a brand new replacement to go with the original that I copied it from."

Yvonne paused, trying to see a flaw in the argument but had to nod in some appreciation.

"Well that's one way around it."

"What else can I do?" he sighed.

Arthur ran ahead, doing his embarrassing faery dancing from one side of the corridor to the next.

Outside it was raining hard. They huddled under a broken bus shelter which had been dented by passing earth-moving equipment, the glass finished off by local boys and scattered around like fragments of ice. The rain thundered on the roof, and burst on the road in millions of atomic-explosions.

"Can't you do something about this? Did you lose *everything* to that cow?"

"Of course I can! And don't slag her off. You didn't know her."

He looked at the sky, somewhat reprovingly. The rain stopped. He was clearly pleased with himself, and gave what amounted to the first smile in millennia.

"Look, if I angle that cloud – so. A delicate tinge of reflected light to see us home…"

"Well you haven't lost it all, then," said Yvonne begrudgingly. "Remember when we were little – the sunsets over the City? Everyone thought they were caused by the pollution from the chemical factory, but *I* knew it was coming from you…"

He looked at her with one majestically raised eyebrow.

"So the Merlin of Strathnaddair is not a complete magical cripple. Even if I *have* lost the wee fellas." He meant the Elementals.

She touched his arm. They walked on. They walked through a wasteland of empty boarded-up houses, burnt out cars, joy-riders and rubbish. They boy continued to walk/dance ahead.

"But could you do anything about this? It's going downhill fast."

"Now hold on. You know yourself that curing Wastelands, when they happen, are *his* responsibility. The Arthur. I do – or did – weather, prophecy, shape-shifting, king-making, and some excellent scrambled egg on toast. But curing Wastelands are *not* part of my remit."

"You caused it."

He went tight-lipped, said nothing.

"What about him, poor sod? What will happen?"

"Yvonne you *know* what will happen! He'll remember who he really is, beat the crap out of someone, organise a gang, terrorise people and impose order, pull some sort of sword out some sort of stone, come to a bad end but save the world… that's the Pattern. Or it was. Don't worry, I'll sort it. The Merlin always does."

Some distance ahead Arthur was confronted by the same small gang of boys, which barred his way. Yvonne would have sorted them but Ambrose pulled her back, to watch. The chance of a confrontation was there, a clear rite of passage, but Arthur backed down, and stepped aside to let the brats past, sneering at him as they went. Some of them shouted back, calling him a fairy. Hart casually threw a rotten apple at the ring-leader which pursued him like a heat-seeking missile, smashing into his arse and sort of hanging there, like …

"Not yet, then," Hart groaned. "Does he know *anything* about himself?"

"He's had some bad dreams lately. He's started reading Malory. Won't talk about it."

Her brother shook his head in scorn, splashed in a puddle, looked in dismay at the generally tattered and battered air of the town. Young men burst out of a nearby pub, fighting and screaming. More cars screamed past, chasing each other. PC Scroop was glimpsed, looking harassed, trying to deal with a bag-snatching, trying to summon up help for the pub fight, trying to get the number-plate of the joyriders. They walked on, they walked on.

"You still want *me* to teach him, don't you?"

"Isn't that what Merlins do? As well as the rest? Besides, if you hadn't played match-maker with me and that —"

"Oh don't start that again! Okay okay… send him round tomorrow."

"I don't know why you have to sound so miserable. I'm not asking a lot."

"It's just I get so fed-up playing second-fiddle. The Merlin is not allowed to have his own life, it seems."

"*Don't!* You never felt sorry for yourself before that bitch came into your life. She robbed you of everything!"

"Shut up sis. Anyway, look…"

Ahead, Arthur was greeted by a gang of girls. It didn't need an expert on body-language or pre-teen social behaviour to see that they all liked him. For once he seemed to snap out of his reverie and give them some concentrated attention. Hart, whose own heart was still ripped out and left hanging somewhere, felt oddly jealous.

"'Dicky Dicky Denches Plays with the wenches'… Is the Once and Future King reduced to playing catchy-kissy this time around?"

"You were 32 before you had your first girlfriend. Remember – all her books were in braille. Anyway, he's a handsome lad. Might be weird, but he's handsome. Got my genes there."

"Handsome is as Handsome does" said her grumpy brother, impersonating Forrest Gump.

The girls passed, giggling and saying *Oooooooo* and looking back at their hunk, admitting that Gwen had been right after all, they just hadn't noticed till she had pointed it out. He was just *soooo* different to the other boys.

They came to his house and paused at the gate. Shuck came out to meet them, and gave Arthur his paw. They could feel the cold from where they stood.

"You don't have to go back in."

"I do. The Merlin must."

"You've turned it into a shrine."

"I have to."

"So that's your punishment for trusting someone not fit to wipe your fat backside?"

"Please… don't say that. I loved her. I *love* her. She's in my head all the time."

Hart went through the gate and opened the front door, pausing at the threshold. He walked into solid crystal. The door closed. Yvonne could hear him sobbing, but what more could she do?

They held the first lesson in Arthur's bedroom, which looked more like a monk's cell than anything a normal boy would have. The bed was neatly made with the blankets tucked into fiercely exact 'hospital corners'. There were no ornaments, no posters, no model aeroplanes, just a shelf of very dull books relating to the Arthurian Traditions. The first thing Hart had done was look under this nephew's bed for the pervy magazines which might prove him normal after all, but the floor was bare, without even any fluff.

"Oh for god's sake read it to me. I know you can. You're articulate when you want to be."

Arthur just fiddled with the book, turning it this way and that.

"Right then sonny, the choice is yours: make some bloody effort or I'll recommend that you're sent off to that Special School. And you wouldn't see young Gwen then, would you?"

One of those things touched a nerve: whether it was the threat of the Special School or the mention of Gwen, but it suddenly seemed as if his distant gaze now slowly focused itself, like a deep-space space telescope suddenly concentrating on something earthly. Arthur looked at the page: one, two, three seconds, then looked up and intoned in a flattish voice without punctuation:

"'Then Merlin went to the Archbishop of Canterbury and counselled him for to send for all the Lords of the realm and all the gentlemen of arms that they should to London come by Christmas upon pain of cursing and this cause that Jesus who was born on that night...'"

"Well that's better. No' bad! But it wasn't quite like that. I *know* what it was like. I was *there* – or one of me was. You make it sound like *Letter from America*. That bloody Malory. I never did trust him."

Hart began to pace around the small room with frustration, remembering. "Oh Arthur it was exciting. It was… big! It was like one of these rock festivals, and me the main act. The Merlin was *never* the drooling old duffer that Malory described. And the women… Oh the women! They were different then – attitudes I mean. You know, as my old pal Geoff 'Chalky' Chaucer used to say, the one thing all women wanted in those days was 'sovereignty', and they'd try every wile to get it, and they went like rabbits! But here in Strathnaddair, now they've got it, what all women want is to feel hard done by, and they moan like chain-saws. Especially as far as their menfolk were concerned. I could you tell you some tales about that, too. But now pin your ears back laddy, because this is how it *really* was…"

Whatever powers The Merlin might have lost, he never lost his memory, or the ability to summon up things from the past that should probably stay in the past. He paced in a sort of figure-of-eight around the narrow floor space next to Arthur's bed, his eyes as glazed now as his nephew's had been, and probably for similar reasons.

"Merlin strode like a panther across the great hall of the Bishop's palace, aware that the ladies' bosoms were heaving with barely concealed desire at his broad shoulders and narrow snake-like hips. He paused briefly, to thrust his tongue down a few of their eager throats, fondled an occasional pert young breast, then drew himself up before the whole court, summoned up all of his awesome majesty and said…"

"Stop."

His uncle came to an astonished halt in the middle of the lemniscate, his mouth sagged open.

"*Stop?* Why stop? I was getting to the good parts, the way it really was. Listen, the truth is Merlin was the main man. The Arthur, well, he was just a little bas—"

"You don't know your Malory," said Arthur, his voice still toneless.

"Hey listen pal, I knew Malory! At least, one of me did. And let me tell you what a prig he was! His personal habits were *appalling* – he had this collection of brass-rubbings which were … well, don't tell your mother."

"I like him."

"Oh well you would! Listen, never take a man seriously who has urine stains on his doublet. And as for his writing style – that was always non-existent. I think he works for the Daily Telegraph these days."

"Read him properly. Then you wouldn't be trapped in the crystal cave that only you can see."

"What do you mean? *What do you mean?*"

Arthur looked at a page in the book again. Blinked, as if to save the information, looked up and then recited it word for word:

"So by her subtle working she made Merlin go into a cave of Crystal and so wrought it for him that he never came out for all the craft he could do and so she departed and left Merlin."

Hart snatched the book from him, and read, in a near panic. "'That was never there before – I swear it. I thought this thing with Viv was just a wee blip! That we'd get back to the Pattern soon enough." He grabbed a book down from the shelf and frantically looked up other sources. "Geoffrey of Monmouth… there it is again, the crystal cave! Robert de Boron… there it is *again*! T.H. White…. the same! Edward Grahl… Joseph Campbell… Walt Bloody Disney! The books have rewritten themselves because of what I've done! I've altered the past! It's true – I'm trapped. It says here 'for all time'."

He sank onto Arthur's bed in disbelief. Uncomprehending. His great weight made Arthur bounce a couple of times.

"How…?"

"We've got a new computer at school. It's got a programme. A spreadsheet."

"So?"

"If you do numbers, and change the last figure, it changes all the other figures right back through. It doesn't matter what went before. They all change."

Hart looked at him with a certain respect at last. "I think you know more than you let on. I think you've been taking the wee-wee out of us all this time."

But Arthur just looked as blank as he had always done. He and his uncle sat on the bed, backs to the wall, staring somewhere into space. Yvonne was listening at the door. They both knew it, not because of any occult powers, but because cigarette smoke was drifting through the large keyhole, and they could smell her perfume, which Ambrose called 'Possession'.

"I've messed up the old and true Pattern," he mused, thinking it through. "I've created a new one. I'm gonna be trapped forever. Bloody hell…"

He suddenly realised that if he was to be saved at all, it would have come through the boy, his sacred nephew and all that.

"Well what does Fart-arse Malory say about me and the Sword in the Stone, eh? Does he give me any clues there?"

Arthur didn't look for this one: "'And Merlin wrought a wondrous —'"

"Oh that bloody Malory… Listen, if I have to be diminished, you at least must try to remember that it was more like this: *Merlin, resting briefly from his marathon love-making sessions with the brightest and comeliest of the damsels in the whole of North Britain, devised a typically brilliant test for the prospective King. The crowds gasped as his tanned, supple and finely-muscled body lifted a mighty anvil onto a stone. They swooned as he plunged a mystic sword into the cold iron. And mothers offered him their nubile daughters when they saw him make the whole impossible object float down the river into Camelot. Merlin! they cried, with shining faces. And Merlin, scarcely having broken sweat, said – he said –* Hey Arthur, I'm giving it some welly here and you're not listening. I'm in trouble, pal. We're all in trouble. Can you not make any link between all these stories and yourself? Can you not see *Who* you are? I'm asking you for help, you little —"

Arthur shrugged. There were street disturbances outside. They had had a lot of those lately. The sky glowed with a couple of distant house fires and the overworked fire crews rushed toward them. Everywhere there was loud and raucous shouting where once they had only had the noise of crows. The people who worked out on the moor were taking over the town when they came into it at night for the pubs, to let off steam.

Yvonne came into the room. Being a woman, and a mother, she was aware that something had happened. Having Ambrose as a brother, she could not be sure if this was a good thing or not. The three of them looked out of the window, into the failing community.

"When you let someone like Vortig into your world then things follow on behind him, like flies to the shite. How many times have I got to say it: Evil cannot create, but it can infect. Vortig has infected us all."

"You were going to stop him."

"I got distracted. If I hadn't been a fat git, she wouldn't have got to me. If I'd been slim and handsome and had a woman of my own, I wouldn't have looked twice."

"It's chaos out there," said Yvonne. "Is there nothing you can do?"

"Chaos needs control. Chaotic forces need a strong individual to deal with them, channel them, balance them again. That's a king's job," he added, looking sideways at Arthur.

The boy had turned away, losing all interest.

"So you've ruined The Pattern," said Yvonne.

"Aye," he said bleakly, getting his jacket to leave. Shuck leaped up from his doze in front of the sitting room fire. If dogs could give looks which could kill, then this beast was doing so now. "The only chance is to have a meeting – a grand meeting of all the Merlins. Trouble is, it can only be convened by one person, and I haven't seen *him* for years."

He slid the patio door open and called Shuck to follow, and was about to step outside when he realised the dog was not moving. Instead it gave a strange grunting noise, as if something was stuck in its throat. A wind began to blow from somewhere and the lights dimmed, grew brilliant, before the bulbs burnt out completely, yet the room was still filled with an eerie silver light coming from Shuck. Yvonne grabbed Arthur and the three of them held each other, their hair standing on end, the tattoos on Hart's arms all alive and writhing and prophesying madly. Slowly, slowly, the dog raised itself onto its hind legs, its very shape changing into a more human form until the figure of the Egyptian god Anubis – the dog-headed man – was standing there in the corner. The figure reached up and removed its dog mask, revealing the grey haired, lined, and very angry features of:

"Wolfy! I mean *Master!* I was just thinking about you! But you knew that of course. *Yvonne!* Stop *bowing!* And all this time, you and Shuck…"

The mask went back on. The two pronged staff was held high. His master's voice, when it came, was metallic, almost tinny. It brooked no opposition.

"Decompose yourself!"

"What – more than he has already?" asked Yvonne, looking at the wreck of her brother.

"I can't – quite. I've lost a bit of… you know."

The creature held out the wand. Hart grasped it, sucked its energies into himself. His body began to shimmer, take on light form. His shape began to break up.

"Now follow me to the Centre."

"Beyond time and space? Into the fourth dimension?"

"A small hotel in Leamington Spa, actually."

Master and pupil faded out through the patio doors, and Yvonne was left to wonder about the burn marks on her carpet.

There was once a tree in Leamington Spa which – the cartographers had determined – was rooted at the exact centre of the land. Little wonder that one of the Lesser Merlins, Aleister Crowley, had been born near there in 1875, or that the Blaise Hotel should be within spitting distance of its trunk. Not that real Merlins spat a lot, you understand, for fear of precipitating natural disasters involving wind, water, and bad hygiene, but such things are all part of the Pattern.

The hotel itself was an old and eldritch affair with tilted roofs, bulging walls, skewed windows and oddly shaped rooms. You could visit a hundred times and never think anything odd about the place; but the plain fact was, when the Merlins were around, the inside was far far bigger than the outside, for it was really an access point to another realm – although the service was often terrible in both.

Any mortal entering the Hall of Judgement, as they called it, would have blinked and shook his head, and wondered if he had stumbled into a hall of mirrors or something similar. It was a large room of banked rows, almost like an amphitheatre; each seat was occupied by a local or regional Merlin, and each one – except for the clothes – identical to Ambrose Hart.

First Wolfy (in his full Anubis regalia) made a regal entrance to a tune that was not dissimilar to the dread rhythms of The Volga Boatman and you could see all the heads bow, slightly and briefly, before turning in unison toward the door from which Ambrose would emerge.

"Come," said the teacher of teachers, the Weaver of the Pattern, looking to the darkness in the doorframe and gesturing with his hand.

Strathnaddair – for that was how they called him – poked his head through first with a sort of *Oh hello!* expression, and then allowed his body to follow, dreading what was about to happen but unable to avoid it. The only comfort he could salvage was the fact that, for once, all those who were about to judge him were fat bastards too. The minute he was fully in the room they roared their disgust, and 168 Merlins with big chests, big gobs, and large quantities of thwarted *mana* could blast the hide from a rhino.

"Lads, lads…" said Hart uselessly, trying to summon from them a response that lay somewhere between pity and forgiveness. But they were all fat bastards, and completely united in their scorn.

Wolfy raised his double-pronged wand and silence fell. The master took off his Anubis mask and you could see the marks it had made on his skin, the sweat pouring off him.

"Hot in there, eh?" said Hart with sympathy but he was silenced also. For a long moment which might have been years or decades or a complete generation, nothing was said, though you could feel the power building up. At last the accusation came:

"The pattern has been altered. The flow has been deflected. The land is unbalanced."

If a wormhole in space had opened up then Hart would have leapt into it head first. There, in the middle of the Judgement Hall, in the very centre of the Land, he lost whatever morsel of self-esteem he still had left, and knew that he was probably the biggest failure in all of recorded history. Including the House of Windsor. One hundred and sixty eight clones of himself were looking at him with contempt. What else could he do but bow his head in shame?

"Is there any who would speak?" asked Wolfy.

The air erupted as every Merlin spoke at once, and you can imagine it was like Armageddon in that room. There was thunder; lightnings flashed from the east even unto the west. You'd have expected the Four Horsemen of the Apocalypse to come riding in any moment to add their own spleen, it was that dreadful. Wolfy raised his wand again and silence fell instantly. He chose one to stand and speak while the rest shifted their bums and settled down to listen.

"Northummerland; The Merlin of Ashington, me. Whey man Ah'm not happy. Ah waz daeing aalright man, things wiz gannin canny until that ugly bugger there started his tricks."

"Look pal…"

Wolfy silenced him. "What is your solution?"

"Whey that's easy man. There's only one thing ye *can* dae. Deal with the source of aall the trouble, and aall his power. Slice his bollocks off."

A close shot of Hart's face might have resembled a powerful seismic disturbance. He went red; he went white; all the muscles below the skin twitched like galvanised frogs.

"Oh you would, *bonny lad.* That's because you've never —"

"Silence! Another. You."

"Zummerzet. Merlin from Baltonsborough here. Lets not be 'asty, Oi say. All this daft talk o' slicing 'is bollocks off! We're Merlins a'ter all. We must take a cool, wise view."

"Way to go friend! Too right friend!" – and he pulled a face at the Geordie Merlin.

"So what Oi suggest is this: without anger, without 'ate, we should simply, well… *rip* 'em off. Off. Just loik that."

And without anger, or hate, he mimed doing exactly that,

and throwing them on the floor, and you could almost see them bounce.

And to see the faces of the other Merlins you could tell they thought this was an eminently reasonable and rational solution: that his balls be removed and weighted against the Truth, as was done with the heart in the Egyptian afterlife.

And as for Hart's face…

The two regional Merlins began talking to each other, making cutting, ripping gestures. The conference room erupted again as all the Merlins agreed, pounding with their fists, and it was a good job the place was insulated or the entire land mass of Great Britain, and probably parts of Brittany also might have slid into the sea. OFF! OFF! OFF! – and Wolfy's wand with the two-pronged end started snipping like clippers, and if Hart had never felt dread before he felt it now.

"Silence! Merlin of Strathnaddair… take heed. This world is unbalanced. The cause is *you*."

"Hey wait a minute, are you saying… are you saying that all the violence and decay, all the disasters, are *not* caused by lead in petrol, holes in the ozone layer, nuclear fall-out, drug-abuse, global warming, E-numbers, and inept social and political programmes, but have all happened simply because I fell in love with a little hairdresser from Penge?"

"Well… yes."

He swayed. He didn't know what was about to happen next. What punishment could you give someone who has messed up the entire world?

"Have you anything more to say?"

"What can I say?" he replied desperately, his voice almost squeaking. "Tell me what I can do!"

"You have your specialist powers."

"But the duplickation goes wrong."

"Duplickayshun – hah! Shite!" – this from the Ashington Merlin.

"Well better than *your* speciality, pal! What was it again? 'Mayking light things dark, and dark things light.' I mean, come on *hinny*, unless you want a black fridge what bloody use is —"

79

"*Think!*" roared their master, and they all sat back, all just a little a-feared of him from their schooldays. "Make the negative become a positive. That which is wrong can become right. Make the fault become a virtue."

Hart felt shaky. This was all too much.

"I don't understand."

"The Merlin of Strathnaddair has to understand. You have stumbled into Retrospect. You have twisted the Pattern and knotted Time."

"And done simply *tewwible* things to poor Tom Malowy's pwose!" cried The Merlin of Brighton, and they all joined in with expressions of disgust, in all their regional accents.

"Look guys, I —"

"Go!" cried Wolfy, putting the Anubis mask on again and pointing in his magisterial way toward the blackness of the door.

Hart was bewildered and sore afraid. He looked around at the ranks of the other Merlins for some scrap of sympathy but there was none. It was the biggest group of stone-faced and unforgiving fat bastards he had ever seen. He turned and walked out, shoulders bowed, the loneliest man in the world.

Without the Merlin's powers of vision you might look in on him and see a middle-aged man on a couch, gone to seed and getting worse. The place was a mess. It had never been hoovered or cleaned for days. The sink was full of plates. The waste bin was overflowing. The rooms hadn't been aired, and stank. No vermin could live in such a place. Even the dog had gone.

With the Merlin's powers of vision you might have seen the whole house as a solid block of ice-like crystal. All of the Elementals were trapped, frozen into place, except for the salamanders who just sort of thrashed their fiery-looking tails from side to side like bored soldiers, waiting for the order to charge which never came. When Hart did move it was with an effort: he felt resistance at every step. Whatever thoughts he had in his head at the time remained in space. So if he was thinking about Viv's body when he stood near the sink, they remained there, in the aether, repeating like an old movie. Which meant the entire house was filled with memories. He walked through them, when he had the strength of will to walk, and it became harder for Yvonne to drag him out, and even harder for him to survive outside. And all this quite apart from the bollocking he had had from the Council of Merlins.

I can't go on, he thought, looking mournfully at the images of Viv which floated – sealed in crystal – everywhere he looked.

The phone rang; after a pause he pressed the loudspeaking button.

"Hello," he said morosely.

"Oh I … I thought this was the Mystic Brotherhood," said the vaguely familiar woman's voice.

"They fell apart. Anarchy was unloosed. It was terrible. The carpets…"

Then came the sort of silence which almost shouted with concern. "But what about Simon the Seer?"

Hart rubbed his temples, his mind on other things. For a moment he had no idea who Simon the Seer was, or had been. Then it came back to him, seeping slowly through the crystal padding of his life.

"Hello? Hello?"

"I'll try and put you through," he said wearily. Then, using the voice: "Simon here. Look, darling, I feel a bit of a fraud. My power is… not what it was. Save your money."

"Don't hang up! Please. Listen. I know this sounds crazy but… I was worried about you."

"Worried? About a phoney — I mean, er, a voice on the phone?"

"Well, yes. You see I c-can *see* things also. But never for myself. For others sometimes, yes. B-but for me, no."

"You have the Sight?"

"Well, more like a feeling."

"Same thing. And what do you feel about me?"

"That you're troubled. Surrounded by … loneliness. That you've b-been, er, thwarted in love."

Hart stretched to pick up the original photo of Vivienne. It seemed to glow. His eyes became damp.

"This is costing you money you don't have, my dear."

"Forget the —"

He hung up. Misery can be all-enveloping. Its indulgence can also give a strange sort of comfort. Sometimes, you don't even want to escape its embrace, and can be almost happy to sit there like Hart did, trapped in crystalline memories. He patted the phone and muttered: "Thanks anyway. Have my blessing, for what it's worth these days."

Like an old man he creaked off the couch and went to Viv's room, which still had all her things in it, exactly as she had left them of course. Even the hair-dryer on a stand had not been moved a millimetre. The crystal was at its thickest and coldest here. He sat on the bed and sank his head in his hands.

Arthur and his mother and his by now dog-rough uncle were in the field where they had last had the picnic, when the hawk had arrived and changed all their lives. The grass was churned up by motor-bikes, two burnt-out cars smouldered and stank of burnt rubber. In the distance, if you stood on tip-toe, you could just see the framework of the nuclear waste reprocessing plant taking shape on the once-bare moors, like the skeleton of a vast animal. Below them, Strathnaddair looked more cancerous than benign, more decrepit than idyllic.

"Listen Arthur, I don't want to put you under any pressure, you being my only beloved nephew an' all that, but it's up to you. You gotta get this sorted." Hart had started smoking again. What harm could he do to his world now? Even Yvonne had agreed, and lit up with him, and they both sat on the fallen tree trunk and puffed away.

"You have to find yer sword," she explained. "I'm bein' symbolic here, love."

"Correction, sis, he has to find a stone. And in that stone will be a sword."

"Which you have to pull out. Symbolically speakin'."

"Yeah, that's right, only you. No-one else will be able to do it."

"Sword," said Arthur, swinging on the tree again, a right little gymnast. "Words is sword is words is sword is words is sword is—"

"All right all right all right!"

"No, son, it doesn't have to be a real sword. Remember it's all symbolic."

"Words is sword is words is sword is words is sword. Stuck in my head, stuck in my head stuck in my head…"

"Oh for fu—"

"Leave it Ambrose."

More joyriders came roaring up, the wheels gouging out the soil, flinging it up like water-spray. There were rare plants in these meadows whose pharmaceutical properties were worth billions, if only they had been known, and were being crushed by Japanese off-road vehicles with American tyres.

"Words is sword is words is sword is words is sword…"

"Let's get him home…"

The Newcomers that Vortig had shipped in from various locations had brought a sense of chaos; the chaos had infected the impressionable. From originally welcoming the influx of foreigners, the staid folk of the town now kept indoors, afraid of the new dwellers on their threshold. Some of the youngsters of the town aped the immigrants. Many small shops were closed and boarded up. The Co-op had iron shutters on its windows and closed very early. Drugs were sold openly at street corners. Sisters were hired out. Used condoms were strewn all over the park. The small services in Strathnaddair were unable to cope.

Yvonne, Ambrose and Arthur made their way through all this, the boy as always dancing some yards ahead.

"Makes me feel old," said Yvonne, watching a fight develop outside a pub.

"Don't think like that," comforted her brother. "You *are* old."

"I'm glad you lost your dog," she said.

"Yeah, I loved Shuck."

"I didn't mean Shuck."

Up ahead, down the narrow street of shops known as The Shambles, three rough and drunken young men were harassing Elaine and Gwen, who had simply been trying to post a letter. One of them had lit the waste bin, another was being sick down the wall of the old post office, and the third was prodding Elaine with a golf club that he had taken from the smashed window display of the little sports shop.

"Look! – a Mashie Niblick I'll be bound," said Hart, who loathed the noble and ancient game, but liked names for the sake of them, as all Merlins do. "'They say his father was the finest swordsman in France!'"

"I know them – that's the girl who's sweet on Arthur, and her daft mum."

Yvonne was one of those females who, when it came to men and their depredations, had no fear. Perhaps she was old fashioned, and still believed that no man would ever hit a woman; perhaps she knew that, as a mother, she could summon rage and strength and ferocity to put anyone to flight; perhaps it was just because she was rough as a badger's arse and could take on any fella.

"Right," she said, throwing down her fag and becoming wild, as all Scots can, for 'the fighting Scot is a Primitive', as Field Marshal Montgomery once said, and you can bet that he had once tried shagging a Strathnaddair lassie in his youth.

"Ah… I think caution is the best option here. I see three exceedingly nasty grown men. Don't let's rush this."

Yvonne gave him a look of disgust. "At least you could look menacing."

"Okay." And he did, and with his wild hair and unshaven face he looked like something from the third circle of Hell, though he couldn't have said whether the change came from the inside out or the outside in. "But sis, look…"

There was Arthur dancing in front of the yobs – who of course are no more than backward boys at heart. It distracted them enough to let Elaine and Gwen squeeze past, where they joined the other two.

"Quick," said Yvonne, seeing them approach. "Sit in the shadows there. You're embarrassing me."

So Hart kicked upright an abandoned milk crate and sat on it, well into the shadows, while the other two women joined them in a curious kind of sanctuary.

The backward boys were amused. It was largely fuelled by the alcohol, but there was also a genuinely absurd air about Arthur as he danced around them, not-quite touching, looking at them oddly, as if he knew something they did not, and never would, half-singing and half-chanting: "Words is sword is words is sword is words is sword…"

"Loony," said the leader with the golf club.

"Thick as a brick," added the vomiter, who felt a lot better now that his supper was on the outside of the post office wall.

While the third one urged: "Go on, Rocky. Hit 'im."

Rocky tried, but Arthur dodged effortlessly, grinning hugely.

Among the spectators, Elaine and Gwen gasped with horror. This was getting serious; Elaine felt personally responsible; she would have tried to intervene but Yvonne held her wrist in such a grip that she winced.

"Hey…" said the latter, nudging her brother.

"Aye… we're near the moment I'm thinking. Are you? You are?"

"I'll call the police," said Elaine.

"*No!*" cried brother and sister in rare agreement. This was good, this.

"Words is sword is words is sword, thick as a brick, thick as a brick…"

"Hit 'im Rocky! I'll hold him! *Ow* not me!"

"I d-don't understand this," said Elaine, and Hart recognised the stammer at once, and sat up, but also slid a little further into the shadows. He didn't want this woman to see him in such a state. But nor did he want to miss this drama.

"In actual fact," he said, in a tone like Dr Snoddy, "quite apart from the anagram, words *are* swords. Words can hurt. They can cut. They can stab."

The would-be attackers were unable to grab him, even though he stayed within the narrow confines of the street. He seemed to be boneless: they couldn't grip. He was incredibly fast: they couldn't keep up. His movements were oddly serpentine, and kept just within the laws of motion and gravity – but amazingly quick.

"Why won't you help him?" asked Gwen, worried about the boy's safety but also aware that something very odd was happening.

"Ah, well. It has to be this way. We're waiting for something. It's to do wi—"

One of them reached into the sports shop window and pulled out a baseball bat.

"Oh dear oh dear oh deary deary me!" said Hart in cod-Indian.

"I feel sick," said Elaine, who didn't really, but felt that it was her duty to feel that way, her being into spirituality and the like. "Please," she said appealingly to Hart, "do something!"

And to his own surprise he was oddly touched by this plea. All right he was a slob, and he couldn't cover 100 metres in much under 10.5 hours, including adequate toilet breaks, but he was very fast over very short distances and underneath the flesh there was still a hard lad who knew how to punch his weight. He stood up and wrenched the bat from the panting young man easily enough, held it behind his back for a second and handed over a duplickated one.

"You're taking a chance," hissed Yvonne.

But still they failed to make contact. Arthur ducked and dodged, weaved and slid, and it could have been orchestrated, it could have been Gene Kelly out there, but without the rain. It was almost as if Arthur existed and moved to a different Time to the rest of them, for he could anticipate their moves before they even thought of them, and all the while he was chanting: *Words is sword is words is sword, thick as a brick, thick as a brick...*

"Brace yerself," said Hart. "The sword. The stone. We're nearly there. Y'see, the 'sword' is the 'words' that we've labelled him with. Sticking in his brain. Autistic my arse. Do it, sonny. Remember, remember what you are inside, remember..."

Suddenly:

"STOP!" – this from Arthur, so powerfully that they all did.

And the boy turned his back on his attackers, faced the heavens and shouted with all the passion that a young boy can summon: "I. Am. Not. LOONY!"

"Ooooooh!" said Yvonne.

"Oh…" said Elaine.

"Rex Quondam, Rexque Futurus!" declaimed Hart majestically. "About bloody time, too."

Lightnings crashed. Thunder rolled. The street lamp above them flickered on, uncertainly at first, with increasing brilliance, until it seared down onto the boy who stood there with his fists clenched and his face in the kind of ecstasy he shouldn't even begin to experience until well into puberty, and his body seeming to shine with an inner light.

Behind him, too stupid to be aware of Myth and Magic, the one with the baseball bat elbowed his way forward and raised it like an executioner, and everyone could see that murder was about to be done, and screams came from somewhere. He brought it down on the back of Arthur's head with all his strength, but Hart had guessed well, and the duplickated bat broke like an egg-shell and left the attacker looking like an idiot.

"'And lo, he brast the spear upon the villains neck!' I never did know what 'brast' meant, did you?" he asked Elaine, feeling the kinship with complete strangers that can often happen in wartime.

She looked at him oddly; but better things were happening out there.

The golf clubber came next, and whether it was because Arthur was distracted by all the Myth and lightnings, or whether he just got lucky, he caught the boy an awful whack across the shoulder, and was about to follow up when a small silver missile shot from behind them all, whooshed past them with enormous speed, and smacked into the man's forehead, knocking him unconscious.

Everyone stopped and turned. It was the gang of boys which had menaced Arthur on his way to school, and the ball bearing from Cooky's catapult which had done the damage. The boys were looking at Arthur – who was now, unbeknownst to them, *The* Arthur – with open-mouthed awe.

"Need any help?" asked Cooky.

The Arthur smiled, and shook his head, and it was a different sort of smile to the ones he had shown until now.

"He's back," said Hart.

"He was never away," said his mum.

But there was one attacker left, and he was nothing if not bold, for courage isn't the sole preserve of the good, nor stupidity exclusive to the brave. He took a knife from his pocket and made a dash for Arthur, determined to avenge his pals in the ultimate way, annoyed that the honest little fun they had been having had gone so badly wrong.

Before anyone could move Hart was on him, and it became a legend in its own rite how the Fat Git moved like gazelle in that moment, grabbed the knife hand and punched the bastard's face so hard it made an impact like the Shoemaker-Levy Comet which everyone filmed crashing into Jupiter at a million miles and hour. He hit again and again until the whole face looked like a ripe tomato, and everyone left standing had to pull him apart as he took out his frustration on everything and everyone. He might be a fat git, a lard-arse, a mound of blubber, an obese, lumpy, round and flabby mountain of flesh, but inside… inside he was *hard*.

There came the silence which is always supposed to fall after a battle. The school bully of Strathnaddair Middle School removed his green cap and handed it to Arthur, and Gwen kissed him, and Yvonne hugged her brother, and Elaine gave everyone odd looks as she always did when linked with matters spiritual, and they all sort of stood there like lemons, coz the Myths never gave much practical detail about what to do next.

"Anyone for a nice cup of tea?" asked The Merlin helpfully.

Arthur, even after he became The Arthur, never lost his inherent strangeness. Despite odd bursts of knowledge which showed that he was still able to access Another Place, he never became as articulate as his uncle or as expressive as his mam. By any standard he came across as something between a cold fish, and a very calculating young boy. Any normal mother would have worried that she had a potential psychopath on her hands, or else urged him to go into politics. But inherent strangeness can go a long way in this world, when coupled with good looks, courage, and unusual skills. Then people start using the term 'charismatic', and spread the word, and if you force others to look at someone in that sort of light, there's no stopping their destiny after that.

No-one, of course, had ever called Hart charismatic. That was the curse of The Merlin – or one of them. All things had to be kept secret; he could never flaunt himself. And on the rare occasions when someone learned of his real nature, it was not so much wonder that he inspired, but fear. And being a fat git didn't help much either. *Fear and Loathing in Strathnaddair* could have been the title of his automythography, had he written it.

He sat in Yvonne's front room, smoking with an almost erotic delight. If True Love and Happiness were to be forever denied him, if he would never have sex with anyone but himself ever again, then at least let him enjoy a good smoke. He was sprawled on one of those fake leather couches which tend to stick to your skin in hot weather and make small farting noises when you move. His sister had just finished cleaning, and, lacking the powers he once had taken as the norm, she did so the traditional way – with an old upright hoover.

"Thanks for bringing me out again sis," he said.

"You gotta learn how do it yourself. It's all in your mind."

"The whole of the manifest universe is in my mind, darlin'. It gets crowded in there."

"You still miss her then."

"Every moment, every day."

There was pre-teen laughter in the kitchen. That is to say it was high-pitched, with a minimum of innuendo, and still had the pure echoes of innocence.

"That's his Council of War, bless him," said Yvonne, putting her ear to the door as always. "They plan to demonstrate against Vor-Tech. Him and Gwen and his little band of eco-warriors."

"He's found himself at last."

"Seems so."

Hart switched on his vision: he could still 'see'. He saw the Elementals which had once shot across his inner realms like quicksilver now just lying about, torpid and lazy, scarcely bothering to move – although the salamanders were, as ever, glowering at him.

Yvonne cracked open the door. Silence shot through it. They might be warriors, but they were also terrified of Arthur's mam.

"Would you like some —"

Then she saw what they were drinking and why they were so merry and burst into the room and gathered the bottles of alco-pops from the formica table. "When yer older, fine – but this is my place and I've got yer mothers to answer to."

Fuming, she came back and dumped the bottles on the couch next to her brother, who watched them clink and roll into the side of his arse, because of his weight on the cushion.

"Eco-warriors," he smiled, almost amused. "They're snot-nosed mindless little thugs."

"Aren't they always?"

Hart shrugged. She had a point. Was Francis Drake a hero or a murdering pirate? Was the very first Arthur of the Britons a Freedom Fighter or just another terrorist burning houses down?

"Let them get on with it," he said, duplickating the alco-pop.

"Yeah but if the whole pattern's twisted, we don't know *what* should happen now. Who ballsed it up?"

Hart poured the duplickated alco-pop into a glass (he hated slobs), sniffed the bouquet, tasted it, registered a certain shock and then offered it to Yvonne, who shook her head.

"I hate the things!"

"Just taste it."

She did so. "It's just water. Pure water. So?"

He stood up and paced. Small objects vibrated on the coffee table as he stumped past. You could almost see the brain cells working.

"'That which is wrong can become right'! That's what Wolfy told me at the Council. Old Wolfy knew! He knew! Listen I —"

The doorbell rang. Something triggered Hart's senses. He remembered that first time when he had answered the door to Vivienne and —

A handsome, olive-skinned boy stood waiting politely on the step.

"Bonjour," he said to Hart with a slight bow and impeccable manners. Yvonne, looking out of the kitchen window, wiped her hands and made toward the door to greet him.

"It's the French exchange student," she said. "I expect he wants to join the gang."

Hart, remembering his Malory and all the trouble caused by the Frenchman du Lac, with his foreign and sophisticated love-making, blocked the door with his mighty frame so Yvonne couldn't get to him. To the small and wary creature before him, he must have looked like the Matterhorn.

"Not this time, sonny," he hissed, so that spittle almost sprayed the boy. "This is for *hommes*, not *omelettes*."

Then he slammed the door in the wretch's face before turning to look in at the gang, hoping against hope that Gwen hadn't caught a glimpse of her Lancelot. If he had to balls up the Pattern, he might as well do it completely.

"Pig," said Yvonne glaring, but not wanting to challenge what was left of The Merlin.

"A very sacred beast, the pig. Now where was I?" he mused, raising the glass of water to the light and thinking hard.

When you have been dumped, you take on the cold vision and frantic beating of Merlins. Your mind soars, it plummets. It enters dark places and sees the object of your love in all those possible situations that hurt most: entwined with another; laughing with another; comfortable and clearly happy with another – for once. And the words – the sharpest you can fashion – come into your mind like swords, but all you do is cut yourself.

Hart could have seen Vivienne if he had wanted. He could have entered a large mock-Tudor Manor and found his way down the mock-ancient corridors to the Great Hall, and seen her at one end of the large table, with Vortig at the other, though it would have gutted him to hear her call him 'Carl'.

"Caaaarl," she teased, oblivious to the waiter who refilled their glasses without needing voice-commands. "Carl Carl Carl Carl Carl Caaaarl…!"

"You're drunk," he said, with a face like an axe.

Vivienne pushed the glass away. It slid across the polished top, spilling the champagne. She leaned across and licked it up.

"J'ai fini."

"Don't say that to a *real* French waiter. It means you've just climaxed."

He may have been a principle of Evil, as seen by others, but he was abstemious himself, would have made a great Knight Templar, Taliban fighter or CIA agent, and was uneasy around ill-discipline.

"Maybe I *have* come. You don't know what goes on beneath the surface, do you? Under this polished table top? How long did it take your eunuchs to make it shine like this? Did your arse-lickers lick this too?"

She giggled. Hart would have recognised that giggle, though not the rest of the performance.

"Enough," said Vortig.

"Enough of me, you mean. You've had enough of me. I make you uncomfortable. I frighten you. You want me to go."

She pouted; she looked hurt. Although she didn't have the range of voices that Hart could muster, she had a protean face. Within the space of a minute, she could seem to be a dozen different women, with a dozen differing expressions. If Vortig had been a bit more human he might have felt a chill of fear.

"I said —"

"You want to get back to rutting among your secretaries like a great stag, hanging their knickers on your horns."

"Look, you did a job for me, but —"

"But now it's finished. And so am I. J'ai fini. *Haaaa…*," she sighed, hands to her head like the Little Match Girl and standing up unsteadily.

"Going back to your lunatic friend?"

Hart might have felt better about his lot if he could have seen her expression then.

"He made me laugh."

"Did he?" asked Vortig, really irritated, because you can accuse a man of being cruel, selfish, lazy or thoughtless, and – by and large – they can take it on the chin. But accuse of him of being humourless and it floors them.

"He did. He was funny. And he had more real power in his little —"

"Little what?"

"I'll show you. I'll show you what he taught me."

She walked up to his end of the table, steadied herself, took up a crystal glass of red wine, drained it, then, with a bit of effort and an uncertain start, she duplickated it.

"I don't want to see that! I wish I hadn't seen that!" said Vortig as ever, turning away as if he had just witnessed open-heart surgery, and him not liking needles, blood, or sharp things generally. He looked around frantically for the butler.

"Bruce! Bruce!" he called, and the man came running, startled by his boss's agitation.

"Bruce, for pity's sake take this slapper away will you? Yes she *is* finished. Come and gone."

The man made to grab her arm but was surprised by her steely strength; she shook him off without effort. He caught a glimpse of something within her eyes – something wild and beast-like – which warned him that his own future was in some doubt at this moment. She blinked. Slowly and deliberately. Once. Twice. Thrice. And then it was gone, whatever the something was, and so had the drunken stupor. Without any help or coercion she walked a straight path to the door, and paused for effect.

"Your time's finished too, Carl. And if you must know, I only ever coped with you by acting 'as if' you were someone else."

Vortig crashed his plates, glasses and exquisitely prepared vegetarian courses to the ground.

"Still," she taunted before making a sweeping exit, "an enchantress has to earn her living somehow…"

If you look at Time in linear terms – and lets be honest, few of us do these days – then a few moments later Vivienne was driving along a treeless and desolate road that probably echoed the state of her soul when, out of nowhere, a great stag crashed down onto her bonnet, the head smashing through the windscreen and only stopping short of her face because the antlers kept it back. Pushing herself right back to avoid this obscene kiss, and sliding down to slam on the brakes, the car and its new passenger slewed from side to side before it came to a halt.

Did Viv know fear then? Or shock? Perhaps a bit. But she had grown too much into her Myth, and too far away from humanity to retain the usual feelings. So she sat there, slumped in her driving seat with her hands still on the wheel and the great head of the stag with its lolling tongue right in her face like some new customer, she looked into its dying eyes and *saw* things…

She saw Elaine on Hart's doorstep, ringing the bell with a nervous look on the muscles of her face but real determination in the sinews of her mind, and she knew – as only a woman can know – that she wasn't there to sell him *The Watchtower*.

Oh no you don't she thought to herself, doing the woman thing.

So she hadn't lost *all* of her humanity.

The thing about great beauty is that it can have a narcotic effect. You can get hooked on it, like the old ladies who drink their Ginger Wine by the crateful, and can't stop, and can't see the problem, and won't drink anything else in any case. Once you have been with someone like Vivienne, anyone else can seem like a dead planet.

That was something of what he saw when the doorbell rang and he found Elaine standing there, twitching a little, as all 'good' people do when they're in the presence of imponderables. Like so many who have a reasonable intellect but little personality she had taken up the easier aspects of New Age religion and bought a variety of joss sticks, dressed in flowing purple, and adorned herself generally with crystals encased in spirals, strange sand encased in little pendants, ankhs dangling from every bit of loose flesh, Indian sandals, henna tattoos on her hands, and wore her hair in such dreads that he just wanted to untangle it, brush it straight, and give her a good shampoo.

Of course, that put him right off her from the start. Many malign thoughts coursed through his brain:

Why do they think it's spiritual? Do they really think it has any effect on their souls? Some of the biggest tyrants in history loved wearing purple! Did it benefit their *chakras? All this crap bears the same relationship to real magic that Roy Rogers did to the real cowboys. Honestly!*

Tetchy or what? Fussy or what?

Yes, that was a *real* curse that Vivienne had put upon him, and real curses have nothing to do with venomous spells cast by bell, book, candle, using wax dolls plus a few greying pubic hairs to make the link. Instead, real curses have everything to do with Beauty as it was, and as it might have been, acting together like thumbscrews on the empty present where it no longer exists – empty but for the hard knowledge that it never will exist again.

So Elaine stood there, bearing a placard which said <u>STOP VOR-TECH</u> in an uncompromising font that had been painstakingly coloured in, the letters now beginning to run because of the light drizzle which had started in the sky and in his soul.

"Your Arthur sent me. F-forceful young man, that."

Hart ran his fingers through his hair. Despite his spleen he wished he looked a bit more presentable. It was a Man Thing before it was a Merlin Thing. He pulled his stomach in but then thought *What's the Point?* and gave up, and sagged.

"So, er, what's the little brat up to now?"

"Oh he's c-cleaning up the streets."

"He's not still got that Mashie Niblick sword-thing has he? I told him about that!"

"Oh no, I mean literally cleaning them up – well, almost. Him and his gang, they're collecting litter. 'Small things first' he says, and… he's shaming everyone into noticing how things have gone wrong. Come and see."

Forgetting himself for a moment he tried to step out, but smashed into that crystal barrier which only those of The Old

Blood could see. He looked embarrassed. This was not a good day.

"Look, er…"

Elaine, of course, could not see the barrier; but she looked past him into the house and saw the myriad pictures of Vivienne.

"That's her, eh? She's very pretty. Yvonne told me all about her."

"Oh I bet she did! Look, I don't expect you to understand, but —"

"I *do*. Love can trap you. F-freeze you to the bone. Sometimes you need help."

Elaine pushed her hand over the doorstep, through the crystal, and toward him. Surprised, he took her hand and found it a very warm hand, and allowed himself to be drawn out. He didn't think she would have the power but maybe she had the warmth instead. Though he didn't notice, some of the plants in the garden – the very smallest ones – begin to show a glimmer of life. *Hmmm* he thought, as all men think when they're appraising a woman. If only she would change her hair, dress differently, lose some of the mystic jewellery, then… *Hmmmm* he thought again.

Elaine seemed pleased with herself. It was almost touching to see. It did wonders for her stammer too. "Merlin moved lightly on his feet for a big man," she said, as if quoting. "The sun caught on his noble features. The crowd gasped…"

Well you can imagine that Hart himself gasped. "Who taught you that?"

"I… I don't know. Just a story in my head. I'm trying to write a children's book."

"You have… hidden depths."

Elaine, like many of the New Agers, was too dim to feel patronised or insulted.

"I do try to see below the surface of things. I think it was Thomas Aquinas who pointed out that b-beauty is when the inner identity of a thing shines forth in its true form."

"Nice," said Hart, who caught a glimpse of the Elementals moving again, but very slowly, and stiffly, as if they had been sitting in the same posture for too long. Of course if his had been a deep soul he might have seized his chance and managed to put the traumas of Vivienne behind him. But The Merlin and Ambrose Hart are not always one and the same, and the latter was dominant at that moment, and all *he* saw was a chance to have sex again.

"M-maybe you could… I mean —"

His destiny hung upon this next second. Would he try to do the things that all Harts have done since time immemorial when they thought they were in with a chance? That is to say, try to get his tongue down her throat, hand up her jumper and her kecks off before she could say Hail to the Jewel in the Lotus? Or would he listen to his Higher Self, as focused through the myth of The Merlin, and exchange mutually respectful perennial wisdoms which might lead to better things?

Well, you can guess the answer to that. He was a man, after all, before ever he was a Merlin, and glands are hard things to ignore. But, for once, hard decisions about a possible renewal of his sex life were taken out of his hands as Vivienne suddenly appeared on the doorstep. In her slinky black dress, black stockings, high heeled shoes and – he knew – nothing else. And what an effect that had upon *his* chakras, eh?

"Hart," she said, and that was all she needed to say.

"Vivienne!" he exploded. "You've come back. I knew you would!"

It was like a strange ritual as Vivienne strolled back into the house, looking nowhere else but at the man, and him standing there at the apex of the triangle in which Elaine formed her own sharp bit but was not seen at all, as if an invisibility spell had been cast upon her – which in a way it had.

"I… I think I should g-go," said Elaine, and she did, and the other two never looked or said a word as she sort of slunk out, doing the tail between her legs thing, dropping her placard on the ground.

"You've come home," said Hart in wonder, as the two of them shared Looks and he heard music again, which might have been Stravinsky's *Rite of Spring*, or possibly Petula Clark's *Downtown*, but he wasn't sure as his brain wasn't working properly because of the overload on his heart.

"Come here, Big Boy," she said, beckoning him with a finger that had more power than any wand he had *ever* seen, while outside the garden went into a slump again.

The next day, outside, dark clouds roared over the town and released their rain in a sort of carpet-bombing technique that seemed to target Hart's cottage in particular, smashing against the windows and the slate roof, and flattening the already demoralised flowers. Hart stood there in his underpants and vest, his brow flat against the cold glass as he had once seen Arthur do, looking out at the dead hawk which lay in the garden with its wings splayed. If he thought he had known despair before, then it was just a rehearsal for that present moment.

There was knock on the door: his sister. He dreaded this moment too: when she could indulge in what is possibly the most obscenely satisfying pleasure ever known: saying *I told you so…*

The knock was a formality. In fact she came straight in, went from one empty room to another, sneered briefly at the state of her brother's bed and faced him, in the sort of classic arms folded and legs akimbo posture that hadn't been seen properly since the Ealing Studios went under.

"She's done it again." Which in some ways was even worse than saying I told you so.

Even a tanned and muscled hunk would find it hard to look appealing in the old-style Jockey Y-fronts; Hart just stood there, less like Olympus and more like a one-man slum.

"She said she loved me, missed me. I made her laugh."

"I bet you did."

"I couldnae help it."

"Yes you could."

Something struck him then. He caught a glimpse, with the very ordinary vision of the sibling rather than the extraordinary seership of The Merlin, how Yvonne saw the situation.

"You don't think I regret it do you? You don't imagine I'm beating my chest in shame? You do! You really *do!* Listen you daft bitch, I would do the same again even if it caused a slow death for every man, woman and child on the planet. Viv was the greatest thing that ever happened to me. I would give up everything and everyone to go through it again. Now, no matter what happens, I can look back and say that, just for once, I – me, the fat bastard that gets blamed for everything – knew the sort of woman that any man would die to have, and felt that someone saw through to the *real* me at last. And she didn't care whether I was fat or skinny, wrinkly or hunky, black, white or tartan, coz she saw through to that wee little spark in here which is ME. So that stupid little cow, as you called her, knew what we ALL should know: inside, we are ALL enchanting. That's me, Sis. I'm not just a Fat Git. I'm The Merlin. And. I'm. The. *Enchanter*. Merlin the Enchanter, have you got it yet?"

She looked away, for he had touched a nerve. Everyone has a Grand Passion in their lives somewhere, at some level, no matter how briefly. Or if they don't, then everyone can feel that they are capable of one, and yearn for one, and feel that their own humdrum lives are lacking, somehow, and go on the quest for something that is quite as marvellous as any Holy Grail; and people get hurt, lives devastated, and fertile realms turn to wastelands – but that is how it must be. Yvonne was no different. She who existed in her role somewhere between that of sybil and slag, knew exactly what dread and barren realm her brother was going through, though she could probably have traversed it a bit quicker.

Then, coz she was a practical sort, she made him wash, then dress. She made him shave. It took all of her force of will to bully him into the slightest action; it was like pushing a boulder uphill. And on the seventh day (for that's how long it seemed to take) she rested.

"Come on, we'll go for a drink. I'll fix you up with that Elaine. She's gasping for it. She's a *real* woman."

He didn't say Yay and he didn't say Nay; largely because he was suffering from that General Paralysis of the Insane that mortal men get from time to time when they fall foul of their women; Merlins are no better – just a whole lot more intense.

She looked him up and she looked him down, and he still looked like crap, but she stepped out of the crystalline force-field as before and tried to drag him outside, but this time it wouldn't yield. She grabbed his wrist with both hands and put her foot with admirable suppleness but shocking inelegance against the doorframe, and heaved with all her strength, but still he wouldn't budge.

"Oh god… she's really got to you this time. Come on!"

"I can't. I can't leave, even with you helping me. I don't think I'll ever leave now. It *must* be true love."

"She must have given you a bloody good seeing-to."

"It was more than that."

"It was *the Merlin* she wanted. Not my big brother."

"I *am* the Merlin."

"You know what I mean. She could have any man she wants. Do you really think…"

"I made her laugh."

"Well, that's what you do when you're a Fat Git."

"Sis…"

"I can't do any more. You'll have to help yourself."

Turning, she walked off down his garden path, and the rotted gate fell off its hinges at her touch.

Perhaps Heroes don't really exist any more, except in Hollywood – which in some ways is just a suburb of Strathnaddair. Perhaps we exercise our own souls so little that we surround ourselves with fatuous needs, so that we end up with something inside that feels trapped, and starts signalling wildly for a Hero to come and cut us free. And of course Time and wishfulness can add a glamour to individuals who, if the truth be known, were never more than murdering little bastards, like Robin Hood, Captain Kidd, Dick Turpin, the Kray twins – or Arthur and his new followers.

His mam was dead proud of him though, and that was all that mattered.

There was no doubt that the boy had, up until then, lived largely in Another Place. Myth and legends are full of stories of men and women who – usually by accident – stepped through bodily into another dimension which overlaps with ours, and who spend centuries – if we look at it etc etc – peeking back into our world and trying to return. Arthur, far from being a lunatic, was probably one of those who got stuck halfway: his body was in our world, but not all of his psyche. In another Age, in another society, he would have been a natural born shaman, and treated accordingly, and that would have been the end of it.

But the other boys of his new gang didn't really understand this. They were in some genuine awe of his new found presence, but – by and large – they still thought him a bit of a loony. And maybe you have to be a loony first before you can attain the status of Hero. And maybe you can't have one without the other.

In actual fact it was Gwen who organised them. Although Arthur was more articulate than before, and able to string insightful sentences together, too often he drifted off into the Forbidden Zones again, and what he said were more like Zen koans than clear statements of intent. Boys being boys, and thus more interested in wanking than wisdom, mistook his obscurity for profundity and just assumed he must be right. Or rather, they did so with a little help from Gwen. She acted toward Arthur like little old lady mediums do with those spirit guides named Chan, or White Snowdrop, or the ever-humorous Irish spirit formerly known as Mick. Plus she considered herself so *lucky* to be seen as so *close* to such a *beautiful* boy as Arthur.

Even so, it was Cooky she fancied. When Arthur wasn't looking, he had a tendency to settle on Gwen like a meat-fly. Cooky was warm even if he was a bit thick; he snogged brilliantly. Whereas Arthur was cold, and seemed to see people as things, plus he hadn't a clue what to do with his tongue – although she was happy to let the other girls believe that he did, oh my *gosh* he did! They were dead jealous; they thought The Arthur was just brill, and what a pity he was taken, and they wouldn't have crossed Gwen, not a bit. Hey, she was young! Given the choice between physical and spiritual perfection or a bit of rough with attitude and a big knob, you can guess who made her young pulses race.

Gwen, of course, had been born old. Right from the start she had a disturbing kind of aura, of the sort that would have branded her jail-bait if she hadn't been careful. She was like an old priestess from a forgotten and bloody cult who was – temporarily – trapped within a young body. She was simply biding her time for the moment, years hence, when the outer matched the inner, and she would have no more use for the male of the species except to offer him up as a scrawny sacrifice. Not so much as pulling a sword from a stone, as of getting fire from a cup. Same sort of beginning.

In the meantime… it was she who organised the litter cleaning, getting those tough young lads to go around with black bags and gardening gloves to protect their hands, starting with the town centre, near The Shambles, and spiralling out. She told the rest it was Arthur's idea, and it actually may have been because he did murmur about centres in decay, and things falling apart, and bins needing emptying, and starting with Small Things… So that was pretty clear, and she had to agree.

The sight of these hard lads and their girlfriends doing such things struck chords and consciences within the adults of Strathnaddair. The sure sign of a corrupted or decayed community is when the children are patently lawless. That is the litmus. When they behave, and are seen to behave, the adults feel safe in their turn. Old people would come out of their homes, Mothers would walk their toddlers again. The forces of darkness which manifest through drink and drug-fuelled yobbishness start to feel uneasy, and slowly withdraw, like shadows before the light. Gwen in her ancient intelligent way understood the essence of this, although she could never have intellectualised it. Arthur, in his visionary mode, might have grasped it once, but he could never have brought the words out in anything but oblique epigrams.

The Merlin saw it all, at once, but by now was too frozen to do anything about it.

"Little bastard," he said, when Yvonne brought him news of the town that was part of his very spirit. He was deeply jealous that the boy was doing something of what he should have doing, in another myth, and another Possibility. There had been a time when life for Ambrose Hart was certain. The mains stages were clearly formulated and almost inevitable, culminating in his death in a bowl of chicken soup at the age of 61. But since Vivienne had shunted him into another possibility, he didn't know *what* to do.

"He *is* a bastard," Yvonne agreed, deciding to take his statement literally rather than critically. "He's also my little boy."

"Arthur was never a little boy." He was being, in a magical sense, literal – but he meant it critically.

"We both know that."

The floor was littered with books, each one dealing with aspects of the Arthurian Tradition through the ages. Big books and small books, paperback and hardback, some of them propped open at specific pages by other books and highlighted with a clear yellow pen, many of them dog-eared and sullenly closed. It made the floor of the sitting room look like a rockery.

"Have you read these?" he gestured. It was an empty question: Yvonne never read books. "It says in this one, that one, and that big one there with all the pictures: 'The King and the Land are One'. Have you ever heard such rubbish? It used to be 'The *Merlin* and the Land are One'. Now that makes sense doesn't it? Well doesn't it? And as I remember, although The Merlin had a few flings he never got trapped, and never revealed his last secret."

He didn't exactly rant, but he certainly touched upon the rave. Yvonne took it all, quietly, nodding as women do when their men go on one, leaving their minds to free to think about the eternal verities of sex, violence, and knitting patterns. And to be honest, she was not a little pleased that this new Pattern seemed to revolve around a new role for her son, who was now twice the boy he had been, and improving daily as far as she could see.

"So the Merlin isn't interested in the Arthur any more?" she asked him during a lull, and his face went through every expression from shock, disgust, mortal insult, until it ended up looking ever so slightly guilty.

"It's just… I'm sick of being a pendant to some Wonderchild. I want —"

"You want to stay shut away in crystal, having your empty visions of your empty little slag, tossing yourself stupid."

"Well… yes. If you put it like that."

"Time is a great teacher. You of all people know that."

"Yes but unfortunately it kills all its pupils."

There was a knock at the door and this startled him. Only his sister knocked, but she was sitting there opposite. Were the batteries in his doorbell flat? Maybe if he duplickated the flat ones the copies would be fully charged?

"It's Elaine," said his sister without looking. It wasn't clairvoyance, but simply a bit of matchmaking that she had done the previous day while their respective children had been busy in the kitchen. Of course she knew the brutal truth that all relationships are based upon the crude and uncertain response known as 'fancying' someone, and Vivienne was a hard act to follow. If marriage partners were chosen on the basis of like, laughter, learning and good conversation then they might stand a chance, and last. But instead it all devolved upon desire.

"I don't fancy her! I don't even like her!" he said, tucking his shirt in, brushing his hair, for he still had remnants of self-respect even if his impact with Beauty had made him a snob.

"You don't know her. Look you stupid git, she likes you. She's pretty, she knows things. Get your sex life back on track, eh?" she countered, her sentence containing two truths, two lies, and finishing with a bit of temptation.

"Give me masturbation or give me death!" he said, using a Voice, and he hadn't done that for a while. "Mark Twain! I'm quoting Mark Twain!" He said in response to her look. Like a light switching on, Yvonne went and opened the door all cheery-like.

"Hiiiiii," said Elaine, her voice sort of starting strong and fading away. "Gosh it's cold in here" she added, worrying if her nipples would stand out. They did. She could have killed them. Instead she sort of folded her arms and tried to look all casual but she was terrified.

Purple thought Hart. *Bloody purple again.* What was that song from the 60s… something about a Purple People Eater? He didn't hear it – the musick was still gone – but he wanted to become the title.

Poor Elaine. In a way, she was one of your perpetual victims. She never had a bad word to say against anyone; everyone crapped on her. Maybe the purple helped hide her bruises.

"She needs your help," said Yvonne, who hated silences.

"My help? *My* help!"

Elaine put some books on the table alongside a bottle of elderflower wine that she had made herself. "I n-need advice about channelling," she said.

"Channelling? Hoh no, wrong man, I only ever watch the BBC."

"*Ambrose*! If only you'd wash your neck I'd *wring* it!"

Elaine blushed; Hart had the grace to look guilty. And pulled his collar up further.

"Oh look, forgive me. If I've lost everything else I shouldn't have lost my manners. *Manners mayketh a Man* said me old Mam," and he used another Voice which was always a good sign, so Yvonne made an excuse and left after warning her friend: "You watch him, mind. He's very clever but his brains can go to his head at times."

It was a noble thing she did there, although her brother would never know. She herself actually fancied Elaine something rotten, for quite specific reasons that she could have written out along with her grocery list. If what she felt wasn't like Hart's explosive *and the dawn came up like thunder* sort, it was certainly as cool and lovely as a crescent moon, surrounded by stars. That sort of love. Not as bright, not so in-yer-face but just as magical as far as she was concerned. She had had men, known men, used them, swallowed and spat – but it was women she loved. For reasons best known to her own myth, her own fear, and the bloody insularity of Strathnaddair, she had spent her life acting *as if* she was something else.

Elaine, *mmmmmm*… Elaine was different.

So, on the basis of a saying which flickered at the edge of her mind beginning: *Greater love hath no soft tart than she who would… something or other…* she left them to it.

They sat on armchairs opposite each other. From his point of view she was glimpsed 'as through ice, frostily'; to her he was a massive presence in a very cold room that needed a woman's touch and some very elemental cleaning.

"You phoned me once. You prophesied for me. You said you had the Sight. What you said was correct. So why do you need me? Prithee tell me, eh?"

"I… I lied. It was Yvonne who told me to call you, and what to say."

"Bitch," he said flatly, aiming it out toward his sister's house on the other side of town.

Anyone else might have got up and fled but she held her ground and he had to admire her for that.

"I know you're into my sort of things, and you were really brill as Simon the Celebrity Seer, I really believed in you. Still do, ha ha! But I know there's something inside me which needs awakening, sort of, it's there I know it, but I can't get it to click."

"So you want me to give you a good clicking."

"Look, I've brought these books, to ask your opinions. There's Carlos Castaneda who I thi—"

"I don't like fiction."

"Oh but it's not —" then she understood what he meant, and put the much-thumbed *The Teachings of Don Juan – a Yaqui Way of Knowledge* to one side.

"Well I've got these two books on Wicca, I really feel that might be the way ahead, because of the Goddess orientation and their Green —"

"You'll get thicker with Wicca. They made it all up you know. I knew the old dear who wrote most of the medieval 'Book of Shadows' on a train ride between Brighton and Cheltenham. Throw them aside."

"Okay, okay, then I've got these two about Spirit Guides. They seem to say —"

"Funny thing about these Guides – and I've met more than a few of them - they can tell you everything about your dear departed Great Aunt Sophie, but if you asked them to give you their names, addresses and dates of birth when they were alive on the earth plane they go all quiet and a bit slimy. Oh listen, er,

Elaine, you haven't got a cigarette have you?"

"I don't smoke. Well, not tobacco anyway."

"Then shall we just have a cuppa tea, and forget these books, because what you're looking for is in here," he said, pointing to his heart, "and the land itself. But certainly not in here" – using two fingers to make a gun to his head. He made his way to the kitchen, struggling through the cold crystal padding which still gripped him, and set about doing ordinary human things with kettle and tea bags. She offered to help, but he said no.

It was the reaction she wanted, really. Elaine was not so crass as to believe that she could fathom the mysteries of the universe with volumes that she had ordered at five for a pound in a special introductory offer from the Book Club. But she did feel that there was something inside her that was struggling to express herself, and knew that she needed some help, some guidance, in making the inner link with the outer.

"So you're not into any kind of analysis then?" she called out.

He quivered. Had he still been directly linked with the dark brooding spirit of the Land instead of just the breaking springs of his armchair, tectonic plates within his psyche might have started agitating, then they would have experienced earth tremors, and violent aftershocks.

"I would rather rip off my own bollocks and chew them into a fine paste than submit to that sort of shite. And that's all it is – reaching into the cesspit and dragging up some lumps and studying them, instead letting it all flow out and be used for fertiliser somewhere. Sorry to be graphic."

She shook her head briefly, it was okay, it was brill, really it was, but then everything was always okay and brill with her sort.

"Thought you might say that, somehow," she smiled, and there was the teensiest tiniest emphasis on the word 'you'.

"Who do you think I am?"

This was an important moment for Elaine, and she felt that herself.

"I think you're a very special man called Ambrose Hart."

Well he couldn't continue being a churlish, curmudgeonly bastard after someone said something like that. Although he did wonder if, in the teasing way that certain Powers had, his old black dog had now been replaced by this purple woman of middling age. He wouldn't put it past them!

"Two sugars?"

"Three."

Hart looked at her again, trying to transmute his original appraisal from a simple *Nah…* to the speculative and possibly approving *Hmmmm* – but it still wouldn't work. He just didn't fancy her. Maybe they could try the Just Good Friends thing that his sister kept talking about, which sounded pretty damned radical to him, even if he was trapped in a block of ice like one of the woolly mammoths they kept finding in Siberia.

"Who is the most spiritual person you've ever met?" asked Elaine, rather hoping he might say it was her, or possibly the Dalai Lama.

"Pah!" he said, making a fake spitting noise. "*Spiritual*. Hate the word! It implies superiority, and asceticism, and phoney intellect. But if you must know it's probably Carl Vortig."

"Vortig! How can you say that?"

"Because he's the real thing. He's plugged into energies even if he isn't consciously aware of his role. He's true to himself. A sensualist, with a very rigid code of immorality. He's a necessary part of the Pattern. As Big Al once said: *There is no Grace, there is no Guilt; this is the Law: Do what thou wilt.*"

"I don't understand."

No, he thought smugly from the kitchen, *you certainly don't*.

He rattled out with a small tray containing two mugs of tea and a wide, discerning selection of biscuits, including one gingerbread man that Yvonne had baked in the shape of her unamused brother with a vacuous face and Smarties for buttons. His guest chose that, and she made it dance around the edge of the coffee table saying:

"Run run as fast as you can…"

He might have been charmed if he hadn't been frozen.

"Okay… you want to learn about magic – *real* magic? Well you're at the right place for that, anyway. But you gotta learn about the Elementals first. Can't do anything without those little buggers."

She smiled, almost seraphically, and the under-functioning,

misfiring Merlin of Strathnaddair couldn't help but think: *If only... if only...* Perhaps he might be able to do the business with her if he closed his eyes and acted as if she were someone else?

Then she upended the little figure, dunked its head in the boiling tea and bit it right off.

Outside, on the moor, many men were having their heads bitten off by their bosses, and none of them would look back fondly to this period in their lives, and they would all have run run as fast as human legs could have carried them, given a chance. Almost without exception they hated working in this bleak, pitiless, cold and empty tract which gave out nothing to them at all, except via Vortig who paid their wages – always in cash. Poor, poor people.

And poor moor. If it had its own personality (and all places have) then it might have been described as despondent. You see the moor had done what moors have always done within the ecosystem; it was actually perfect in its moor-ish ways: reliable, strong, simple and uncluttered; eternal. And yet this youngster called Humanity – who had once taken vows to be partners – was doing new things that it didn't like at all.

A huge sprawl of huts had been erected for the workforce. Strange languages and customs rent the air, and much hatred. Great areas of land had been torn open then filled with concrete, to provide foundations. That hurt the moor. It was like having the skin peeled back. More than hurt, it just didn't *feel* right. Plus creatures had been disrupted and killed, plants murdered, energies twisted. Steel girders were now rising to impossible heights where once there had been the cozy old standing stones doing their business in a pipe-and-slipper sort of way, which they had done for thousands of years without fuss, and with supreme effectiveness.

If Vortig felt any of this angst from the land beneath his hand-crafted shoes he didn't show it then as he leaned back on the bonnet of his Range Rover and had his picture taken by the fashion photographer Cheryl Peril for a glossy celebrity magazine which would tout his eco-credentials and maybe push him toward a knighthood. She angled her shots so that none of the havoc around them could be glimpsed; she would angle the text likewise.

"Beautiful, beautiful," she said, for where she stood her gaze caressed Vortig first and then cruised out over the open hills, free as a bird. Whereas from his point of view the young woman with the expensive cameras who chewed the end of her long hair to stop it flicking into the shot, was framed by the rising Gates of Hell.

She snapped away, smiling, wondering if he was going to jump her afterward, and if he would object to her femidoms. She didn't like them herself, much, but it made a statement about her independence, and that kind of thing was important to her. Especially with someone like this: the sort of self-made man who worshipped his creator.

"You can't take a bad photograph Carl, did you know that?"

Carl, who was sterile, knew that what she said was true, although his right profile was definitely the weaker one so he angled his face accordingly. He knew everything about himself. Self knowledge was everything.

"Any requests?" asked a man named Dave who wore a yellow hat on top of a long head which might have provided templates for the Easter Island statues. He was holding his angle grinder at a most suggestive angle indeed, letting the world know that if anyone could grind then he bloody well could. Until he came onto the moor he had worked in a small artists' collective that created more in the way of spleen than collective profit. Thanks to Vortig, he had never been so well off. As he looked at the little tableau around the vehicle he was thinking that he would give his right arm for five minutes with a tart like that. He meant Vortig: he was gay.

"Yes, David. Make it look like me," he said, and the man took a *hard* look at his boss before he began cutting into one of the fallen stones.

The moor winced, but no-one felt it.

There did come a time when even the most placid and sheep-like individuals in Strathnaddair had phrases floating through their heads like: *The Time has Come*; or *Something Must Be Done*; and more usually *This Can't Go On*. Normally they would have heard these phrases in something approaching the lively Voices of their Merlin, which was the same as the voices of their conscience, but now the words just thudded through them any old how. If, as Hart liked to say, Evil cannot create but it can infect, then people can be infected by Conscience too, although it is usually a lot less fun. It was actually Elaine and Gwen who organised the meeting in the little town hall, and Arthur and his gang who put up the crude posters all over the town advertising it. It took them almost an hour to clear broken glass from the floor, and to put out the folding chairs in nice neat rows so that the place would be ready in time. Arthur and his merry men sat along the back, imagining they were bouncers, ready for any aggro, all of them looking toward their strange leader for the lead.

It is said that the reputation of power is power itself. Perhaps, like mothers who see what positive things they want to see in their mad and bad sons, Arthur really was just a boy existing on the fringes of autism rather than a misfiring Divine King. Perhaps, among the boys of Strathnaddair, the Pattern had been so damaged that The Arthur, the Once and Future King himself, was little more than the image they projected onto him, and the real hero was a potential within each of them, teased out by Gwen in this instance. On the other hand Arthur knew all their birthdays, and the day of the week on which they occurred, and what days they would fall on up until about 3002 if they wanted to know that far – which they all did. That was just *soooooo* cool.

"You ready guv?" asked Cooky, who did have strong loyalties despite his stronger lusts toward Gwen.

Arthur gave him one of his eerie violet-eyed smiles, as if he knew things that were beyond all telling, and couldn't be expressed in words. So when he sat back and folded his arms, real casual like, they all did. When he tapped his feet, so did they, but not so obviously.

Hart didn't come of course. He sat at home, watched his videos. Or rather he sat at home and put his videos on and looked in their direction, but saw little beyond Vivienne.

Yet perhaps he had managed to teach Elaine something in the little meetings they had in his cold house, and show her that magic and spirituality were nothing to do with costumes, incense, chants, crystals, ostentatious rites in the cornfields when the moon was high, and all to do with something inside. 'The more you say, the less you are,' he had told her. Certainly she had a new confidence; and perhaps he had started to change her from the outside in, because she had dumped the purple priestess robey things she wore like a renegade hippy and now looked quite presentable, up there on the low stage which up until now had never held more than a few folk bands and talent shows. In fact, although Yvonne and Gwen were up there with her, trying to chair the occasion, she was coming in for an awful lot of stick.

"Vortig has *saved* jobs you silly cow!" shouted one. "If he hadn't appeared —"

"*Vortig* closed the cider factory!" she said.

"You don't know that!"

"But *he's* responsible for all that going on out there!"

"*What's* going on? He brings money to the town! Stick with your bloody dolphins!"

"Nuke the dolphins!" cried one of the lads, and there was coarse laughter from the crowd, not all of whom were against the development, and some of whom had been paid to agitate.

"But he's brought in all these foreigners. They shouldn't be here."

"They're political refugees from oppressed countries. He's giving them meaningful work until their visas are sorted."

"They're wrecking the town."

"That's just fascist propaganda. We should welcome them more, make an effort, not be so bloody insular. The world doesn't begin and end at Strathnaddair."

Well actually it did, but that was an arcanum they had yet to learn – if ever.

Perhaps Elaine realised then, amid the anger and the anguish, the true nature of The Arthur's two-edged sword: the odd fact that do-gooders invariably do a lot of harm, while those bent on evil can often – to their astonishment – end up creating good. Although in her Buddhist days she had long adopted the policy that the Middle Way is Best, she was learning now that when you decide to stop balancing on that fence, it is not always obvious which side will do you the least harm.

"Don't you care about what he's doing to the moor?" she asked despairingly. "That's our lungs up there. How many times did you play up there as kids?"

"Nuke the whales!"

Soon the hall was like Hart's head after Viv had dumped him: it was full of voices, male and female, every age, every opinion, all expressed with louder and louder venom, and if there was a truly low point in the long history of Strathnaddair it was then. Elaine sat down in despair. Arthur started to look twitchy and the other boys felt a bit embarrassed. Yvonne, who was not best suited for this sort of thing despite her acid tongue in more personal situations, put her arm around her friend and hugged her tight, and tried not to gasp. While Gwen – she went out by the back door for the cavalry.

Love can be like cancer: the uninvited guest. It can take over, destroying all the good cells, and the only treatments can involve hair loss, sickness, and radical surgeries. When it gets that far then you know for certain, like Hart, that it's True Love. Elaine, bless her, was no substitute for Vivienne – but then neither had she tried to be. In fact, although Hart had taken a certain delight in being admired for his mind, and his myth, the very contrasts merely served to increase the ache he felt: Viv was young, Elaine was old-ish; Viv smelled like Spring, and Elaine reeked mysteriously of witch hazel. It was no use pointing out to the daft bastard that he was middle aged himself, no oil painting, and reeked of dreadful manly things, because he was fully aware of his hypocrisy. But Viv made him feel as he felt himself to be *inside*: young and sexy and thrilling. With her he could work from the inside out. But Elaine… that old boiler just made him look at himself as he really was: another old boiler. With her he had to look at himself from the outside in. And that was a difficult view to make. There were parts of himself he had never seen in years.

Gwen was in the room with him. That troubled him greatly, though he couldn't have said why.

"You look dreadful," she said. "I don't know what my mum sees in you."

Nor did he. But he wasn't yet at the stage where he could be glad that she saw anything, for amid the hovering images of Vivienne there were many straws that could be clutched. He shivered. Gwen sniffed around and opened a couple of the windows to let some air in. She ran her finger through the dirt.

"After the first seven years it doesn't get any worse," quoth he from Quentin Crisp, falling back on the Prime Directive of every fat git: when in doubt, go for the cheap laugh.

"They need your help," she said, and if he had had the strength to think about it he would have noted that she said *They* and not *We*. As if she already knew that she was part of another myth, a later mystery, which only occasionally overlapped with his.

"Why should I help?" And if she hadn't felt a sense of urgency she might have been aware that he asked *Why* and not *How*.

"Because you're the Enchanter."

"No *the Merlin* then?"

"They're not always the same."

He looked at her hard.

"You're very old for your years, Gwen, eh? Derived from *gwenhyfar* – hence Guinevere. Which means, according to one translation 'white shadow'. Do you know that you *must* be Arthur's 'white shadow'?"

She said nothing. There was a steel about her that was oddly reminiscent of Vivienne.

"Give me your hand," he said, and she did, and he held it, and it was just as cold as his lover's had been. She withdrew it, but not quickly.

"You still haven't given me a reason to help you," he said, feeling vaguely guilty.

"Because you're not just a fat old git, you're The Merlin. And because you're The Merlin, you have to help The Arthur. And being a Merlin is all you've got left."

"Cheeky bitch!" he snapped, but he couldn't fail to notice that there was a touch of Yvonne in her too.

"Your magic is crocked. You can't run, you can't fight, and you're only great in your own stories. Even your dog left you. Without your Arthur you're nothing."

"Hey it's nothing personal, as far as I'm concerned. I'm his uncle, I love him. Well, as far as anyone *can* love a prepubescent, sword-wielding solar hero. But as for my life and his being eternally tied…"

"If you can't be the Merlin you're no use to anyone."

"What do they feed you on! So what are you saying? That I should top myself?"

"You may as well. You already smell like rotting flesh."

"Ah that's just microwaved turkey burger."

"You'll just sit there being no use to anyone, and you'll die in your chair and —"

"Well thanks for your honeyed words! Then it's true – I'm no use to anyone. Gwen, look, I know you mean well but you're too young to understand. Besides, they're all laughing at me out there."

It was her turn to snap.

"Laughing? They're not laughing at you. Even the coolest, handsomest guy in town couldn't have pulled that girl. They're thinking there must be something special about you. They're thinking you must have… oh I don't know."

She was right, too. Whether it would sink through his thick hide in time was another matter.

"I'm going back to the hall. Me and the lads are going to take some direct action. If you won't do anything, we will."

She upped and went without another word. He recalled that Vivienne had done it that way too, strangely enough.

Gwen the precocious jail bait – did she appeal to some dark and dire passion within him? Is this how she planned to draw him out of the crystal – not with invective but with subliminal prick-teasing, like some occult Lolita? Of course we expect heroes such as The Merlin and The Arthur to be above such human peccadilloes as fancying them young. We expect them not to have small, mundane emotions, or the tendency to masturbate when the Holy Grail wasn't around. But although he couldn't, for once, speak for The Merlin, it was quite certain that the very human Ambrose Hart was deeply moved by young Gwen at that moment. It troubled him more than he could say.

Then he felt even worse. He felt guilty and useless and flabby in more than merely corporeal ways. A dirty old man, in fact. He sat there and brooded for what might have been an Age, if he had been completely locked into mortal cycles, then got up to get a scarf from his wardrobe, stood in front of the bathroom mirror and twisted it around his neck as if he might strangle himself, feeling the pressure on his airways and muscles.

It's a strange thing about mirrors: when you're of the Old Blood, and you stare into them too long, your face changes, mask after mask slips on and off until you don't know who you are or who you're looking at any more, except that they are parts of yourself. And then it stilled, and there was no reflection at all, and he knew it couldn't go on any more.

Ambrose Hart, he whispered to the nothingness. *You are a stupid, stupid BASTARD!*

The mirror cracked. The little house shook. He just felt so angry with himself, with Vivienne, with Vortig, Gwen, Arthur, Yvonne and all the manifest universe if truth be told. But most of all with himself. He raged, he fumed, he pounded the washbasin and knocked it off its frame, and he only stopped when he noticed that, on the shelf where he kept his toothbrush, the salamanders were on their feet and grinning wickedly, waving as if they were the best of friends at the last. Not only that but the gnomes, sylphs and undines were all over the place, shaking off their torpor, coming out of their paralysis, and he realised with astonishment that the crystal had dissolved – melted by his new-found fire perhaps. He sniffed the air which came in through the windows Gwen had opened, then went to the front door, moving easily through the empty atmosphere for once, not dragging his feet and shivering. Across the frame was a last barrier of crystal, like a hymen. He pushed his hands against it, harder and harder, and with an audible crack it burst and fell into a fine snow-like dust on the front step. At last he knew that the house was just a disgustingly untidy house and not a cell any more. Turning to look back inside he saw the Elementals as they had always been: soul-less little creatures that were given shape by his imagination, but very real, and doing what Elementals always did – all over the place, and in a most annoying manner.

"Hey lads, I might need your help in a minute. Don't go away."

He looked back out to the wrecked garden, Then he sniffed his armpits, and glanced almost fearfully at the reproving features of his mum, who surged out of the picture which had hung skewed on the wall for a long time now. He straightened it, but couldn't make eye contact with her.

Gwen's words echoed in his head; he knew he had to finish it.

No-one – *especially* a Merlin – can ever recover from True Love that quickly. In fact he never would, and no matter what positive things might happen for the rest of his life, there would always be a part of him giving that *cri de merlin* which the old romanticists described so aptly but which they could never have known themselves, unless they too had been completely shafted.

It was strange walking through the town by himself. He felt like a deep sea diver without the heavy weights on his feet. As if he might stumble or float off at any moment, caught by the currents in the strange world he now traversed.

You couldn't have said the songs came back to him spontaneously. He had to force them along. Try to get a synergistic reaction going. Why is it though, when you're in a party and someone tells you to sing a song – any song – that your mind goes blank. Even the least musical, most tone-deaf individual must have about a million tunes in his memory bank but none of them come. Or none of the good ones.

"Bless your beautiful hide!" he sang, clutching at something from *Seven Brides for Seven Brothers* which forced itself absurdly onto the surface layers of his mind; and although it exercised his lungs on the empty, battered streets, it didn't awaken any great forces within him. Still, he felt a lot better in some ways. His long hair was clean again, and he was now fastening it back into its customary pony-tail with his best elastic. His boots gleamed and his jeans had been freshly laundered only yesterday by Yvonne, who must have known things as usual. He wore a plain shirt of heavy denim, open at the neck and his trousers fitted him better than they had ever done. At least he had learned one great lesson: if you want to lose weight, then fall in love with someone half your age, have her dump you, and spend the next thousand years eating almost nothing at all. The pounds simply fall away!

Mind you, he was still a Fat Git, but the True Love Diet had lost him nearly two stone, and he was grateful for that much at least.

When he got to the hall there was a right old battle going on – at least on the verbal plane. And it didn't need a top-notch clairvoyant to realise that physical violence was likely to follow because Vortig had hired some of his own likely lads to make their presence felt in the usual chaotic way.

No-one can really know what went on inside Ambrose Hart as he paused before the double doors of the hall, knowing that this was a crucial moment, and wondering whether he still had the balls. He put his palms flat against the wood and could feel the anger vibrating, with occasional interjections from Elaine and Yvonne that did them both real credit, it really did. Did he *really* want to enter that room as the Fat Git who had been dumped? Could he *really* win them over in that role? What about the thugs?

Come on lads, he thought, looking to the north and south, to the east and west, and then above and below, trying to enlist all the help he could from every direction. *I need some welly here.* The elementals were all around, sparkling like jewels again; even the salamanders were on his side for once, now that they had found a merest hint of inner fire.

He thought of his favourite film *The Outlaw Josey Wales.* He narrowed his eyes, put his shoulders back, tightened his pony-tail as a gunslinger might adjust his holster and heard the words in his head: *Hell is coming to breakfast…*

Now if he had wanted to seduce Elaine, he probably could have had her on the table there and then before the astonished multitude, and she wouldn't have worried about Safe Sex at all – and all this simply because of his entrance. It wasn't a good, confident entrance: it wasn't even a grand entrance to a trumpet fanfare: it was a magnificent entrance, even if he said so himself – as he would do many times over the years to come.

The doors crashed open like thunder. Plaster was shaken from the ceiling. This was not to do with any occult powers but purely because the fat bastard was also very strong, and the door hinges had been oiled not that long before. He didn't enter the room, or push his way in: he exploded into it. And best of all, if there were any Powers still watching over him, then they ensured he got his Voices back in full.

Everyone stopped what they were doing. Even the thug who had lifted up his chair to crash it down onto the loudspeaker. Arthur, give him his due, was on his feet and about to dash forward and intervene but Hart put his hand on his shoulder, and winked. It spoke volumes, that wink did, and Arthur being an autistic savant read them all at once. The Merlin's words filled the room without need of any microphone. After all, the voice-box had had a lot of practice from doing *le cri* every moment of every day for aeons now.

"A deathly hush fell upon the crowd," he declaimed, "as he strode majestically into the room. Nubile wenches gasped and strained their necks to see this great natural athlete. There was not a dry seat in the house."

His confidence rose; it soared. A right little cracker had her back to him, long black hair tumbling over her perfect shoulders. He rested his land lightly on one of them and leaned forward, irresistibly: "Pausing only to stick his tongue —" But the right little cracker turned at that moment and revealed herself to be an octogenarian with pebble glasses and no teeth, who grinned alarmingly.

"— to er, stick his tongue, er, firmly into his *cheek*, he faced the adoring masses and said: *See you, Jimmy!*"

With this he ripped the chair out of the man's hands and head-butted him into oblivion.

"Now… the rest of Vortig's little arse-flies – clear off. Let me talk to some *real* people."

To his surprise, the rest of the thugs picked up their ring-leader and did just that.

If it had been a film then the whole hall would have burst into cheers, the collective power of the Common Man would have been galvanised, the thugs would have been overwhelmed, the grannies would have turned their knitting needles into weapons of mass destruction and they would have roared out to storm the citadel of evil. But Strathnaddair hadn't had a cinema for years, not since it burned down after showing John Boorman's *Excalibur*, when some outraged individual had been heard shouting 'It wasnae like that, it wasnae like that!' – so they all just sat there stunned, and perhaps just a bit embarrassed.

"Welcome back," said Yvonne, as Hart approached their table.

"Hi… good work Elaine – no really. Really good work. I'm proud of you."

"You can't show your powers," his sister whispered. "You know that."

"I intend to use my natural wit and charm."

"Oh hell…"

"Bitch."

"Bastard."

Hart took the stage as if he had done so all his life – which in some ways he had. Silence descended upon the hall like a Mexican wave, apart from one who managed to mutter:

"Not another bloody fascist."

"Look pals, I'm not one of your airy-fairy, greeny-weenies. I eat lamb kebabs, tuna caught with nets, and every E-number known to man. I *know* we need jobs, and that Vor-Tech looks as though they might provide them out there on the moor. But honestly, the land beneath is unstable. It'll ruin this area forever, if they don't stop building soon."

"You don't know that!" cried a perfectly reasonable Angry Young Man who was more concerned about paying his bills than imminent global destruction. In fact, there were times when his bills were so fierce that if anyone could have guaranteed imminent global destruction he would have cried with relief.

"Oh but I do," said Hart, ever the reasonable one these days. After all, some of the greatest politicians and philosophers in history had been Fat Gits.

"How?" asked another, a spiky-haired Sixth Former named Jools who was determined to get the Strathnaddairian equivalent of a Socratic dialogue going.

Hart looked back at his sister. He knew that, in some way, he had to show himself.

"In the same way, pal, I know that your watch has just stopped, that you've got 'Barry' tattooed under your crab ladder, and that you took 47p from your mam's purse this morning".

Jools looked like the fella in the horror movies who is first to see the Creature. His mam in the row behind leaned over and slapped the back of his head.

"Hey that's… that's Barrie with an *ie*… it's an old girlfriend, not a —"

The Merlin smiled at his sister. "I've not lost it *all* then!"

"Go for it!" cried Elaine, and he gave her a smile too, a gorgeous smile, because she really did look much nicer in clothes more suited to Laura Ashley than The Lady Babalon.

"You see, I can… *see* things. *Know* things."

"Bollocks!" cried a thirty-something man in a creased suit that looked slept in.

"And I can see that you've just had a 'dear john' letter on… pink – yes pink paper, that is now stained with your tears, and that your guts are tied in knots. And you think that if you can get a good job with Vor-Tech she'll come back to you."

121

Dead silence. He had 'em by the short and curlies now.

"But look outside… look. It's falling apart out there. If Vor-Tech bury nuclear waste in that spot, the radiation will get into the water table, the ground water. *See* it, all of you. See the deformed animals and babies – like Chernobyl. See the suffering and dying. The ruined town, with 80% of the people dead within a decade. See the empty houses and broken streets. See the small child, wandering the ruins, calling for her mother…"

A bit over the top, perhaps, but that's what prophecies are all about: the wide expanse of Cinerama with all the attendant popcorn, rather than the small 14" television screen in the corner.

"If I wanted to hear twaddle like this, I'd go to the spiritualist church!" said the vicar's wife, who was upset that her husband hadn't done something like this, and who would soon give him the hell that he personally had long since stopped believing in.

That last hurt. The Merlin looked pained, mouthing the last two words as if he'd had a slug on his tongue.

"It won't fall apart if we'd just allow Vor-Tech to create some wealth for the community."

He didn't hear who said that. It didn't matter. All the voices were one voice, all the people were one peep. He and the Land were – almost – one again. He picked up Yvonne's bottle of coke, turned his back like a conjurer, duplickated it without anyone in the audience seeing, gave the copy to his sister and asked her: "What's it taste like?"

"Piss. You're still crocked."

"Listen, Vortig and his company can create *nothing!* But all of us here have become infected."

Well they didn't like that. Call them stupid as much as you like, but call them scabby…

"Look I didn't mean that, sorry, sorry… Please, listen. Okay? Y'see this land, and all of us in it, are one. We reflect each other. Out there on the moor, and within us, there is something which is like First Love, pure and beautiful – and so very fragile…"

"What is he on?"

He remembered Vivienne. When he and she had been One. He started fiddling with a pen on the nearby lectern, unconsciously duplickating one after another, until – eventually – his hands were full with them. Not everyone noticed, but the few who did went very silent indeed.

"Can you all remember when you first fell in love? How pure and true it was? But with all those enormous energies underneath. And how we set our memories and deeds in that area like standing stones?" His voice was very soft, his own voice. It seemed to float over the heads of some, and descend like dreams. There were those in the audience who could soak into his memories, and have their own knowledge of Beauty evoked, pulled into the present, and set before their own mind's eyes. They sighed and felt they were with him all the way even if, at one level, they hadn't a clue what he was talking about.

Not everyone felt the same:

"Oh for god's sake!" cried some, who had never known the sort of shagging that he had known, and were getting up to leave coz they had pizzas in the oven and wine to chill.

If he had had any more experience of public speaking he would have pressed home his attack then, got bigger, stronger, even more over the top. Instead he started daydreaming again, for Vivienne was like a drug that was still in his system. The room became cold. People started to shiver.

"Ambrose…" said Elaine gently, who had noticed the slight tremors in the jug of water before her.

"Ambrose…" said Yvonne raspingly, who was also studying them.

It was his sister's voice which reached him. He blinked, came back from the lovers' grove, turned and studied the jug.

"Bloody hell!" he said. "We might be too late!"

If you could have changed shape and dived into that water, into the centre of those ripples, and dived down and down toward the epicentre of the disturbance, you would have been drawn far below Strathnaddair, down through the strata, into an area below the moor and your own subconscious where energies beyond understanding writhed and agonised like dragons. And we would have necessarily seen them like dragons because our minds need to grasp at things, and clothe them accordingly, just as Hart personalised the Elementals. We would have been appalled by the struggles of these winged and terrestrial serpents and tried to rise to the surface to avoid their coils, and then found ourselves emerging onto the moor, surrounded by the massive girders which speared down where once the stones had stood, and perhaps given an embarrassed nod to the crude statue of Vortig that someone had made not long before, with especial care given to the arse.

Hart saw all this, and then returned, and the ripples in the jug were getting more pronounced. He saw the blank faces of those who remained in the hall. He saw the hawk stooping outside the window, and was troubled to see Arthur shaking his head in frustration or disappointment or simply as a kind of condition-related tic, and then slipping out the side door with all the youngsters following him.

"Aye, well, maybe wit and charm are not the Merlin's strongpoints in this century."

He looked at the clutch of pens in his hand, all of them dud, then handed them to his sister.

"Listen folk, you lot do as you want. But I'm off to confront them on the moor now. If you want Strathnaddair and your own souls to go down the tubes, that's your choice. But we don't *have* to let it. That's all I'm saying."

Well this time he didn't make an exit to match his entrance, but neither did he slink.

"You made a right pig's ear of that!" said Yvonne, following him outside.

"Very sacred beast, the pig. Or it was…"

Behind him, left in the hall, the young man with a tattoo under his crab ladder was still being slapped by his mam, and protesting his innocence on all counts.

The great lorries thundered past, sucking the air after them, doing dreadful things to the sylphs. Overlooking them all, on a broken telegraph pole, a solitary hawk peered down, shifting its grip from one claw to another.

"Where's Arthur?" asked one mother.

"Where's Gwen?" asked the other.

"Where d'you think?" said Hart, because they all knew the answer. "They'll be tying themselves to some damping rods if we don't stop them."

"Look," said Elaine, pointing to the line of children scurrying over the crest of the steep hill toward the site. "They'll get there before us."

Hart looked at the hill and looked at himself.

"Come on," he said, jumping into the road to flag down a lorry, standing directly in front of it with the bulk and confidence which suggested it might come off worse if the driver didn't do an emergency stop. He did, and their ear-drums ached with the shrieking of the powerful brakes. There was an antler mascot on the grill which Hart quickly duplickated, waving the copy to the driver.

"This has come loose, pal!"

The driver wound his window down and leaned out to thank him, and was shocked when Elaine and Yvonne piled in the passenger side.

"Well hello…" said Yvonne suggestively, doing the tarty thing that men liked fake blondes to do.

Then the driver's door was wrenched open and the man pulled out by Hart, who jammed the false horns onto his head as he sat, dazed, in the middle of the road. And it might be a funny thing about men, but it was astonishing how happy Hart seemed to be when he climbed behind the wheel, as if the trauma of Vivienne was wiped out at once now he had the chance to be a real lorry-driver instead of just a cuckolded failed Merlin.

"Wow," he exclaimed, showing off his rapture, as if the knowledge and conversation of a juggernaut's dashboard was something genetic – which it probably is. The Merlin looked around at the controls with boyish wonder and awe.

"Hey, what would that arsehole Malory say now, eh? He'd say: *Merlin was wonderly wroth. With a single bound he leapt upon the mighty charger and smiled as he felt the surge of the beast between his legs…*"

"You'll love him when he talks dirty," said Yvonne, nudging her friend.

"Hey girls, forget the magic… in my next life I want an HGV licence."

"That might be sooner than you think. Anyway Ambrose, you havnae driven since Boney M broke up."

But he was off and on one, as they say, pressing the accelerator and making the engine race. "*And lo, Merlin put spur to the beast and said… er, steady on lad.*"

The great lorry jerked forward, stalled, and he started it again, revving wildly. He put his head out of the window and said to the still-watching hawk:

"Can you take a message? *You* know who. Say, oh… well try… *HELP!*"

The great beast roared off down the street, watched by its real driver who sat there on the pavement with the naff horns on his head as if it had been a really great party which he couldn't *quite* remember.

Inside the cab, Yvonne leaned over and said to her brother, quite seriously:

"You probably have to die, you know that."

"Sis… I'm dead already."

Then, looking around the dashboard and fiddling with the buttons and spinning the enormous steering wheel he added: "But I think I'm in the Elysian fields!"

Somewhere in that world she inhabited that was neither here nor there, neither real nor unreal, the enchantress Vivienne bathed in a pool that was surrounded by exotic plants, fed by bubbling streams and warmed from above and below, so that it steamed slightly. She stopped swimming and trod water when she saw a servant approach, a young man with broad shoulders, tapering waist, and a perfectly fitting uniform that suggested he belonged to some comic army in a harmless realm. He carried a golden tray on which was a lavish blood-red cocktail and a silver mobile phone, which was ringing incessantly. Without a word he flung the device toward his mistress who rose from below the surface and caught it, like the Lady in the Lake had one caught Excalibur.

He only did it so he could see her naughty bits, and she was more than happy to oblige, for he would never get closer to her than that, or see more of her human nature than a mythic tease.

"He's out," came Vortig's terse words in her ear.

She smiled and did a backstroke to the side of the pool where the servant offered her the cocktail from the tray. With her free hand she duplickated it.

"He can't be. He loved me far too much."

"He bloody well is. And by all accounts he's leading a mob toward the site!"

"He obviously knew more than I thought. Oh bless…"

"I'm told," said Vortig archly, "it was the love of a good woman which saved him."

Vivienne stared back into the water, brooding, remembering. The water seemed to boil. Down there amid the bubbles, blurred and shaky, she caught definite glimpses of Elaine.

"Get my car…" she said to the soldier-boy, climbing out in a jealous rage and throwing her phone into the steaming depths of pool.

Back in the truck, Hart was beginning to get the merest hint that life could be fun without being The Merlin. He bounced in the driver's seat as if the roads were terrible, which they were certainly not.

"'Poop Poop! Poop Poop! Make way for the magnificent Toad!' *Wind in the Willows* y'know! Toad's wild ride! Have you read it?"

But the two women were hanging on for grim life, and one of them was beginning to have the strongest notion that ordinary life as the merest mortal could be quite appalling.

"Faster!"

So he did, and the machine careered frantically along the narrowing road, scattering anyone and any creature in its path, and any Buddhism that might have remained in Elaine's soul was bashed out of it now.

"Hurrah!" quoth Hart. "Hurrah for the wonderful Toad!"

"Bastard!"

"Bitch! Seriously Elaine, if I ever founded a Merlin School then *Wind in the Willows* will be compulsory reading – or at least one chapter in it."

"I know: Piper at the Gates of Dawn."

"Aye," he said, looking at her with sudden respect. Could common interests inspire the mysterious quantity known as Fancy? Could her respect for him inspire lust?

"Anyway," she continued, holding tightly to Yvonne's hand, her thigh pressed hard against her friend's for balance: "Anyway the toad's a sacred animal as well – I think. But listen guys… I mean, Arthur and Gwen, they'll be okay?"

Yvonne, who was suffering a mild delight of her own just then, replied with an uncertain: "They'll… yes they will."

"What do you mean?" asked Elaine sharply, because being a mother meant that there were times when she could drop the flakiness.

The lorry swerved to avoid the body of a stag; they clutched at each other in an almost obscene embrace.

"She means," shouted Hart above the engine noise, "that because I've cocked-up the whole Pattern, we can't be sure *what* should happen now."

Elaine was suddenly anxious. It was not a game now, and something far more than a Wild Ride – and she'd had that from Gwen's father years ago. "I thought it was all —"

"Look – they'll be all right. I stake my life on it. The Merlin of Strathnaddair promises you. Get out of the way!"

This to a cluster of yellow-hatted drones.

"Really, don't worry," said Yvonne, patting her friends cheek and doing some hard thinking. "Arthur's with her."

"Yes… yes he is. She reckons he's invincible."

Hart raised his eyebrows and pulled a Face, and only his

sister and a few Elementals (clinging onto various sympathetic artefacts for dear ur-life) noticed.

Vortig drew near the site from a different direction. He looked out of the darkened windows and saw the children running riot, overturning everything unstable, smashing everything smashable, swarming like the rats of Hamelin with not a pied piper in sight. They weren't heroes, not really. They were little bastards using a Cause to indulge themselves in villainy. It could have been an old people's home they were ransacking, the pleasure would have been the same.

"I'm getting too old for this," said Vortig to his chauffeur. He looked at the young woman's reflection in the mirror. "Do *you* think I'm too old?" he asked her earnestly as he smoothed his aquiline face, and thought about some more surgery, or another dose of Botox.

"You know I don't."

The car drove on slowly, through a series of fantastical metal columns which looked far better than the old stone circle had ever done, but which were oddly like one of Hart's duplickated items from the post-Viv era: they were false: they skewered the Land and didn't work with it, and the Land knew the difference.

"Kids today, eh?" he mused, watching them scale the ladders like evolution in reverse. "What are things coming to?"

The sky was darkening as the lorry stopped. Inside, the two women looked shaken and shattered but Hart was still revving the engine, as high as a junkie with a needle in his leg. Ahead, the gates of the complex were forbiddingly closed, with nervous men in front of them who were as worried about the man they had just admitted as they were about the little bastards who had just stormed in, and you daren't hit these days, and you daren't even *look* at them oddly in case the police and the Social Services come around.

"Ambrose don't!" pleaded Yvonne, who had seen all the films and knew what he was about to do.

Elaine, who was ever the optimist, suggested: "Why don't we just say: *Hey guys, let's talk, let us in?*"

But the man who had brought them from the world they knew to the very gates of this world they didn't know, wasn't listening. The more he revved, he more he got into his role, and the more the Elementals took on power – and they were getting a right surge then, no mistake. He put on the radio and something Heavy Metally crashed around the cab and made him dance in his seat.

"The world held its breath," he said, in a Voice that might have graced the Old Vic. "Merlin, laughing at pain, shrugged his powerful shoulders and smiled. A single beam of light pierced the clouds and shone on his moment of glory…" And as he said that a single beam of light did just that, and the women said *Ooooh!* and felt a bit happier that they were in the hands of The Merlin just then, rather than Ambrose Hart. "Meanwhile Thomas Malory, trapped in a time-space conundrum, saw himself at last as the po-faced, pederastic plagiarist he always was – and it brast his heart. *Hey Merl*, he cried. *Respect! Main Man!*"

With a last rev and a blast of the horn the lorry surged forward and crashed through the flimsy gates sending men, hats and metal flying before ploughing to a stop amid the churned earth, before the somewhat malformed statue of Vortig. A small security guard – the same John Horne who had tried to stop him when he had entered Vortig's factory – came running up.

"Why didn't you just ask? I'll probably have to pay for that gate! Oh it's you again…"

"Hi! Listen don't worry pal, we've come to sort things out, if you understand my meaning. Have you met my sister?"

Yvonne did the dutiful thing and waved, but she was still holding Elaine's hand and pleased that her friend was making no attempt to let go.

"No *you* listen. You won't just walk out this time. Not not with your kneecaps intact. The boss is here, and he's got some very nasty friends in this compound."

"Ambrose…" said Yvonne, worrying about her son. What would the foreigners do? They had strange practices, some of them, starting with infanticide and ending with necrophilia.

Hart touched her arm, trying to send her awesome energies of reassurance, and also to stop her hitting him with it.

"I've sent for Uther. I need him."

She looked as if she had been smacked in the face by one of the hub caps that Cooky was throwing around like frisbees.

"You bastard! No one has ever *needed* Uther. Some of us – *some* of us! – have had Uther forced upon us, but no one has ever *needed* him."

"Who's Uther?" Asked Elaine, who heard it as Yootha, and thought it might have been some eldritch sub-space Being that real magicians evoked from time to time. Which was probably about right, if truth be told.

They both ignored her, though Yvonne did squeeze her hand a bit with what muscle power she had left after that confession.

"Sis, you *know* why I did that: you needed his seed. That's part of the Pattern. So what if I made him look like Elvis instead of… oh, this is *not* a good moment for this argument. Where is he? Where *is* he…?"

"If *I* knew I would tell the Child Support Agency. If they can't find him, no one can find him. Uther owes —"

Arthur's face appeared in the windscreen, dangling down form the top of the cab. He had heard everything from the open window.

"Uther's my dad," he stated in that irritating way he had, as if the world didn't exist until he had made a declaration about it.

"Yes, he's your dad," said his mother.

"Dad's coming," was all The Arthur said in reply, sliding down the windscreen and then over the bonnet in a way that seemed to insult all known laws involving gravity and boys.

"I'll be keen to see what he looks like *this* time!" said Yvonne with a withering glance at her brother as she and Elaine got down from the lorry and squelched in the mud it had made.

Vortig walked so carefully over that mud that he sort of glided. He had a lot of his 'cousins' with him by this time, one of them with a crowbar hanging loosely by his side. When Hart saw him, he got out of the lorry and stood his ground. All other activity stopped. Even the brats ceased being brattish so they could come and watch a good fight.

"So, Ambrose Hart again. As I live and breathe. Unless you have a small miracle up your sleeve these Santa's Little Helpers you've got can't stop me. This is all meant to be, and you can't stop it."

"As it happens…" said Hart, holding up one finger in such a way that those in the know expected to see laser beams shooting from it, or lighting drawn down to it. Instead there was nothing. Nothing at first, that is. Nothing at *normal* sonic levels. Then one by one the people in the crowd heard a distant roar, growing louder, shaking the ground. The workers looked at each other. The foreigners, who had had enough of being demonised and were quite ready to smash a few heads – especially the fatter ones – started to look anxious.

Now there really should have been a fanfare when The Dragons arrived. Not with a flap of leathery wings and a surge of flame from their massive jaws, but via their Harley-Davisons, gleaming and steaming, engines revving, leathers glinting menacingly, all features of every rider obscured by their helmets, so that they came like medieval knights to the rescue of their True King, and every one of them was Errol Flynn. They didn't stop all at once, but they rode around and around in sequences, like formation flying, weaving exotic patterns which churned up the mud even more, and got everyone filthy, but those who were on the side of Right and needed some Might, didn't mind at all. And then they stopped, in a sort of phalanx before Hart and Vortig, leaving just enough room to let a very ordinary motorcycle and its sidecar squeeze through.

The passenger in the side car, when he stepped out, was clearly smaller than the rest of the bikers. Puny might be an adequate word, although someone once described him as being like a crow without its feathers. When he removed his old-fashioned helmet and goggles he was almost bald, the lumpy mass of his skull decorated with wisps of grey hair which fluttered in the breeze. His face had an inherently convex appearance as if some mighty power had, at birth, squeezed very hard on each ear. And all finished off with slightly unfocused eyes and the sort of teeth that you would never want to poke a spoon between, never mind your tongue.

"Uther," said Hart, nodding, who knew what lay beneath.

"Ambrose," came a very high voice in reply. "I believe I am in your debt."

Yvonne approached him with disgust. "When you came to me that night you seemed so… but afterward… so I wasn't dreaming. *Ambrose!*"

"Do not blame him," said Uther in a stilted voice. "I did ask him to change me. When I did see you first, I did have to have you."

"Uther Pendragon you slimy little git, I —"

"Sis! Not now…"

The rest of the people – the natives of that realm – might have been aware that destinies were being unfolded, and Patterns being formed, reformed, or just unravelled, but when you're an Outsider and all you want is to finish the job and go home, then the principle of Time being Money will always come before that of Sacred Kingship. That said, Vortig's henchman walked up to the biker leader swinging the crowbar in a manner that would have made anyone else back off; but whatever he may have looked like on the outside, Uther was a man of steel, or the Dragons wouldn't have followed him.

"Hey Carlito," Hart called to Vortig. "Tell your golem that if he values his — ah, too late!"

To put it in technical terms, Uther kicked the shit out of him. If you liked that sort of thing (and Elaine watched with a horrified but almost erotic fascination) then you had admire the sheer ferocity of the smaller man and create epigrams along the lines of: *Inside every wimp, is a Hero flexing his muscles.*

They all piled in then, on the bikers' battle-principle of *All on One and One on All*, and young Arthur was in there with the best of them, wielding that pipe like he should have been wielding a sword in another story of another realm. Really, he could have been done for Grievous Bodily Harm but then again these were illegal immigrants and none of them were going to complain, and all of them determined to give a good reckoning of themselves if they now had to go back home concealed in the back of Vortig's lorries.

During all this, Ambrose, Elaine and Yvonne did what anyone with any sense should have done: they hid behind some oil drums. Gwen and a lot of others were there too, mainly children who realised they were out of their depth. And while her mother was enjoying a happy sort of guilt and watching cosmic disturbances on what used to be the moor, her daughter slipped away to do disturbances of her own, coz it was really good this, and she could get a taste for it, and Arthur was fantastic with that lead pipe.

Vortig strolled over to them as casually as if he'd been walking through a park. You had to admire him – and Hart did.

"Hi, Vorty! Give up yet?"

"Impressive. But too late. The lorries still come. The men still work. Your biker friends won't have a lasting impact. Oh! But I have a friend of yours to see you."

It was the best of sights, it was the very worst of sights. His heart leapt and fell at the same moment, if such a thing were possible. Vivienne stepped out the back of Vortig's car and you should have seen her smile as she walked toward Ambrose. It was just like the old times, all over again.

"Oh Christ. What can I do?" He looked toward the skies as if he might find an answer there, and back toward the enchantress. "Not again," he said, starting to shiver. "No. NO!"

"Merlin. Big Fella. Come here…"

Generally speaking, the most powerful spells cast by the most powerful people in the Universe are quite easily broken with the aid of simple piece of lead piping. All you have to do is smash it against the side of their head as hard as you possibly can. That's what would have happened if Elaine – bless her pacifist heart – had got to Vivienne first. As it was, something quite serious started to happen underground.

They knew this, even without seismological equipment, because great silver spumes of steam suddenly shot up from the earth, making columns in the darkening sky. Cracks appeared in the ground, like snakes. Some of them developed in large fissures from within which dragon-lights twisted and turned.

"This is all your bloody fault," said Yvonne, helpful as ever. And he didn't even call her *Bitch* this time because he was in mortal fear, and he knew she was right, and anyway he had Vivienne to attend to; if the end of the world was imminent, he wanted just one more go in the remaining minute.

"Viv, I —"

"Remember yourself!" cried a powerful and oh-so familiar Voice from behind which stopped him dead. He spun on his heel, slipping a little in the mud, and saw the familiar figure of his old teacher, removing his Anubis-mask like a crash-helmet of his own and looking at the proceedings with distaste.

"Wolfy! You've come to help!"

"You have to do it yourself. This land is your responsibility."

"But what can I do?"

"You've been told. It's in the nature of our present powers. The false can become true, the true become false."

"We've been through this before and I still don't … look, I'm sorry, help me. Please."

The magus sighed as if he had never known a Merlin so stupid, and he probably hadn't.

"You have created a Retrospect in the Pattern. You have woven events into a Converse."

"Well excuuuuuse me! But — "

"Look at what is, and think of what should be. The secret is in your stones."

"Oh leave my boll—"

Then he looked all the girders, and saw that they resembled a corrupted stone circle. Like something which had once been right and was now wrong. Like the coke turned into piss, and the pens turned into useless tubes, and the good computer turned into a dud.

He understood. He brightened. Even Vivienne was forgotten in the chance to make amends, which says something about guilt and duty being greater than lust and love.

"Do I have enough power?

"You will have help…"

During all of this Elaine suddenly realised her daughter had gone missing. She found her quickly enough, lying unconscious in a puddle, with a great gash on her head where a flying hubcap had sliced into it. She called for Yvonne, and Yvonne was there.

"Get help!" she begged, and Yvonne went.

She found her brother grasping one of the largest steel uprights on the site.

"Gwen's been hurt!" she cried, pulling at him.

He wasn't aware of anything but the cold metal under his hands, and his mission. He could feel Vivienne behind him but he wouldn't look, daren't look, just focused on the task in hand, and it was probably the greatest and hardest thing he had ever done.

"Look lads," he said to the Elementals who were in their element amongst all this, "I've gotta do a last duff duplickation like no-one in history has *ever* duplickated! And if there's any salamanders among you who've felt insulted by me in the past, then please accept my humblest and fieriest apologies – and get cracking!"

"Ambrose!"

The site shook, it trembled. How much was seismic disturbance and how much was the magic was hard to say, because you couldn't separate the events. In reality – whatever *that* might be on the fringes of a place like Strathnaddair – it was probably the Land itself intervening. It had surely had enough of being prodded and poked by these humans and their Merlins who acted like nicotine patches. It was time now to remind them that the true power on this world was not Man, but Weather and Earthquakes.

The land shook, and made Hart's knees tremble for all the wrong reasons. The sky turned a sort dirty red colour that was matched by his face. The world shot through with flecks of light and lightnings and his thoughts were doing similar. And even though Yvonne was trying to get for help for Gwen, simply because she loved Elaine, she couldn't help but be impressed at the sight of the metal structures dissolving into the aethers and being replaced – slowly, rising like mushrooms – by the standing stones.

And the metal column which he had caressed and duplickated was now a large menhir, inside of which was another Merlin. As he looked around the circle and its avenue, each of the stones contained a Merlin. The one beneath his hands peered out somewhat disgruntled and said:

"Lissen bonny lad, Ah'm not daeing this again!"

"Ashington!" Hart cried, kissing the other on the forehead. "You won't have to."

"Just divvn't torn aroond and ye'll be aalright."

Hart knew what he meant: Vivienne was behind him, tempting, and if he had had one long glimpse of her it might have been a different story.

"Aah can see what ye see in her, if it's any help."

"Thanks. It is."

And it was. He clung to that other Merlin like he was a lifebelt, and didn't dare turn.

All around him the metal structures went, and the stones returned to their rightful places. Things can really happen like that in places like Strathnaddair, and in our own psyches, if you can use your power rightly, and you don't let your head rule your heart *too* often. He only came back to the exact present when young John Horne appeared, carrying the unconscious Gwen toward Vortig's car and breaking all the basic rules of First Aid.

"She's going to die," said Vivienne calmly, and with a certain amusement. It was probably the best and worst thing she could have said in many respects, because it gave Hart the sort of anger which acted like an insulation. "Oh Ambrose don't be such a grouch! You know she is. It was you who taught me 'Only a life can pay for a life.'" She said it in his accent. She was taking the piss. She had always been taking the piss. He grabbed her by the wrist, but she was even more amused. She liked it rough.

"Ooh… you can't hurt me. You still love me. Deep down…"

"I don't," he lied. "On the best day you ever had you weren't fit to tie this little girl's shoelaces."

"That's about right," she admitted. He had always liked her honesty, too.

"Ambrose!" cried Elaine in a panic. "We're losing her!"

"I've called an ambulance," said the guard, with great and commendable calm. "Just hang on!"

Vortig was impressed by the lad. He made a mental note to offer him promotion when all this was over.

"Get it over with," he told Vivienne.

"Come on then" she taunted. "Let's see what The Merlin can do to *me*." She put her other hand on his chest and he began to feel weak again, it was delicious, it was a drug. He dropped her wrist in despair and just wanted to sink into her gaze.

But…

"Howay bonny lass," came a deep Geordie voice from behind her. "Ye might be able to torn one a these soft scotchies inside oot an upside doon, but what aboot me, eh?" This from the merlin who had stepped out of the adjoining stone.

"Ashington!" cried Hart, with conflicting emotions: the male spider, enjoying the sex, actually might not want anyone stopping the female from biting his head off during it.

"Strathnaddair. Ah think Ah might be able tae help here."

Vivienne looked stunned to see two Merlins before her. Two identical Fat Gits is never an attractive sight.

"Can ye remember what me remit is? Me special talent? The one ye sneered at?"

"Maykin' bright things dark and dark things bright…" said Hart, intimating the accent.

"An' if Ah remember ye said as weell" – imitating Hart's accent this time – 'Honestly pal, wha' bloody use is that…?'"

The Merlin of Strathnaddair nodded his head in shame.

"Not sae fast, pet!" cried the Merlin of Ashington, grabbing Vivienne as she turned to flee. She writhed in his grasp like a serpent, which in way she was, at heart. "Lissen, hev ye ivver seen yer dark side? We've aall got one. Some canna handle it, but ye hev tae meet it some day. Right, Strathnaddair?"

Hart nodded, having some idea of what might happen. He looked away, not wanting to meet Vivienne's pleading eyes, and felt treacherous. And then Ashington did that thing with the energies which expressed his own idiosyncratic power, and it felt to everyone as if the time/space continuum had just received a hefty kick, knocking it sideways, and when they looked up, there beside Vivienne was her own shadow self – a seething, spitting vampiric, ugly and scarred creature of darkness and pestilence. We've all got one, though not necessarily in that form. People like Elaine, for example, can spend their lives denying its existence, and often the very last lesson they learn is how to confront it. In contrast, all Merlins are aware of this, and one of the first lessons they learn is how to confront it.

"No..." said the bright Viv with horror and disgust.

"Say hello tae yerself, hinny. Sometimes that's the hardest magic of aall."

The two Viviennes looked at one another; the dark one smiled, the bright Viv shook. She might have learned an awful lot about magic and the mighty all-embracing forces of the universe and the soul of Man, but she had done bugger all about her own self. The creature which had ridden Hart so hard and far, and which had drained him of his essence along with his sperm, ran off screaming with her own dark twin following hard behind, slavering and howling like a bitch in heat.

"Thanks," said Hart to his own double.

"If ye ever want a black fridge someday..."

Then he stepped back into the stone and was gone.

Of course none of this helped Gwen, who lay dying while they waited for the ambulance. Ambrose hadn't realised how serious the situation was, and in truth couldn't have done much even if he had. They were all clustered around the young girl, and even Arthur was looking tragic as if he'd found his soul at the last.

"Ambrose, please…" begged Elaine, clutching at his sleeve. "I'd do anything. Anything." She wanted his magic too, just as ardently as Vivienne had done, but for a different reason.

Yvonne could see what was going to happen.

"Ambrose… only a life can pay for a life. You know that."

He did. He of all people did.

"Gwen…" Hart bent over and touched her brow, gently, very gently, whispering so only she could hear, whispering to her spirit, drawing it back to him like the hawk.

"You're free now, and I know what it's like, how sweet it is. You set *me* free, remember? But I want you to come back. You have to come back. We all love you. Come back, come back…"

That sort of thing hasn't been done much. The balancings required, the exchanges, were simply enormous. But then Hart was a bigger man than he was a fat git, and if you could have held onto your mind when he swapped his life for hers then you might have seen the world shimmering, like it always does in films when they have a flashback, as Hart created the sort of disturbances in the aether that they had just felt from the tectonic plates in the earth. It went dark. Very very dark. The darkness at noon sort of thing. Something was happening, though they knew not what.

Then the sun came out. When it came out, at that very same moment Gwen opened her eyes. When they had finished hugging her and weeping and hugging and weeping and hugging some more – especially Yvonne, who was giving Elaine a *right* good hugging – they eventually noticed that Hart was nowhere to be seen.

It was like the aftermath of a great battle, but without corpses: the sound of the wind across the heather, the occasional crow making its harsh noise, and lots of people amid the stones looking at each other. There was no Hart, Vivienne, Wolfy, Dragons or any of the other Merlins, either.

Vortig stood there looking bewildered. Even the statue was looking less like him now, and more like the original standing stone. It was as if he had had a petit mal and when he came to everyone was looking at him. There was the sound of a car horn. He shook his head and watched the small convoy of expensive vehicles bump and jolt across the virgin heather, stopping in front of him. The first person to get out was the Politician who had once been in his pocket, as the Elementals had once been in Hart's.

"Why have you brought us here Mr Vortig? Frankly I don't see the point."

"This is…" his voice tailed away when he looked at the large stone which no longer looked anything like him.

"This is a protected site."

"But will you not consider…" he pleaded, stalling for time, though he couldn't have been specific if pressed.

"Mr Vortig," said the Politician in tones which implied that he would never get to be a Sir if *he* had anything to do with it. "This is a World Heritage site. The Stones of Strathnaddair are sacred! Perhaps not in your country, but certainly here."

"I just don't underst—"

"Oh God! That's all we need!" said the lackey for the Man from Westminster. "And you with an election coming up!"

A group of locals approached carrying banners and banging drums. Local television cameras were following them. They looked really angry. Really *really* angry. The Politician, who knew himself as a Man of Power and Influence, almost ran toward them, knowing also that the power and influence was something that he held in trust for them.

"Please! Please! You have nothing to fear. As your MP I can assure you that the land is safe. My party has always championed green issues. I've had strong words with Mr Vortig and thrown his application out. End of story."

Vortig climbed into one of the cars, all his huff and puff gone, his brain having temporarily seized up. And while the local mob harangued these people who had scorched over the moor in their Range Rovers for no useful purpose, Arthur and Gwen, Yvonne and Elaine made their own troubled way out of the circle and down the long ceremonial avenue which looked as if it had been untouched for aeons. They felt sick. They were totally dumbfounded. They hadn't dreamed it: they still had the physical scars. Then:

"Hi!" said Hart, stepping briskly from behind one of the stones. "Now, do you know anything about computer spreadsheets? Y'see if you make changes to one item —"

The women mobbed him of course. Arthur was too old for that.

"I thought you died, you bastard! Only a life can pay for a life!"

"I did, you bitch! At least *The Merlin* did. Me, boring old Ambrose Hart lives to fart another day."

"So you're not a Merlin now?"

"Look…"

He took a pen, tried to duplickate it, but nothing happened. The others didn't know whether to look pleased for him or disappointed.

"How will you cope?"

"I'll just have to use my rapier-like wit and rugged charm."

"Oh hell…"

They paused to look back upon the cheering crowd and the small convoy of vehicles which somehow gave the impression of slinking off. As they passed, the politician gave a regal wave. Vortig in the back furrowed his brow; there were things in his life which he would have to confront soon, or go mad.

"So what will happen to Strathnaddair?" asked Elaine, who didn't care about anything now that her daughter was alive and well.

"It will find another Merlin. Every place has to have one. The circle is never broken."

He offered the two women an arm, and they each took one. They laughed and approved as adults do, to see young Arthur and Gwen – two perfectly normal children with thoughts of homework and heaving petting on their minds – walking on ahead, holding hands.

Strathnaddair returned to its idyll. The small emerald vans from the cider factory drove carefully along the roads. The pavements were level and clean. The greenery was as green as green things could possibly be, and people were polite as they always were. And where was Ambrose Hart, the former Merlin, during all this?

He was in the little Job Centre.

"I have to ask you some questions," said the Advisor, who smiled at the large and familiar figure sitting opposite, glad for his sake that he had found a woman at last. That sort of thing couldn't be easy for a fat git like him. The woman in question, Elaine, sat next to him holding his hand. He held it tight, hoping the warm, loving flesh would drive away the cold remnants of Vivienne's touch. "First, your full name please?"

"Hart. Ambrose Hart." It was odd saying it like that. He didn't have to hold anything back, any secret role or mission or myth which would qualify such an ordinary name. No longer did the silent words echo in his mind: *I am The Merlin of Strathnaddair.*

Outside, Yvonne happened to pass by and saw them both sitting there. She gave a wave, concentrating it all on her friend, hoping that her fingers would flick her love in that direction. Elaine took her hand out of Hart's and returned it, shyly, somewhat troubled for reasons she dare not yet admit.

"Occupation, or previous employment?"

"Ah well, that's a bit of a *long* story…"

Not far from there, on the bleak and haunted expanse of moor, young John Horne who had been a Security Guard in another realm of possibility was exercising the large black dog which seemed to have attached itself to him. He stopped to look at a bird of prey, fixing it with his binoculars.

"I do believe that's a merlin," he said to the dog, which almost nodded. Quite uncanny the beast was. Seemed to have been with him forever.

As he walked on he saw something glinting in the heather. It was a beautiful silver bracelet, set with glittering black stones. He picked it up. He flicked it high into the air, and it flashed in the sunshine. As it fell he caught two bracelets, one in each hand, identical.

He smiled.

He knew.

He patted the dog.

"Hmmm… my turn now, eh?"

CPSIA information can be obtained at www.ICGtesting.com
Printed in the USA
BVOW071733290112

281621BV00003B/1/P